Dear Reader,

I can hardly believe that it is almost twenty years since I wrote my first Harlequin book. The thrill of having that book accepted and then seeing it on the bookshelves—being picked up and chosen by readers—is one I shall never forget.

Twenty years seems a long time. So much has happened during those years; so much has changed and yet so much remains the same. The changes that we have all seen within society are, I believe, reflected in the books we, as Harlequin authors, write. They mirror the changes that take place around us in our own and our readers' lives. Our heroines have changed, matured, grown up, as indeed I have done myself. I cannot tell you how much pleasure it gives me to be able to write of mature—as well as young— women finding love. And, of course, love is something that has not changed. Love is still love and always will be, because love is, after all, an intrinsic, vital component of human happiness.

As I read through these books that are being reissued in this Collector's Edition, they bring back for me many happy memories of the times when I wrote them, and I hope that my readers, too, will enjoy the same nostalgia and pleasure.

I wish you all very many hours of happy reading and lives blessed with love.

Penny Jordan

Back by Popular Demand

Penny Jordan is one of the world's best loved as well as bestselling authors, and she was first published by Harlequin in 1981. The novel that launched her career was *Falcon's Prey*, and since then she has gone on to write more than one hundred books. In this special collection, Harlequin is proud to bring back a selection of these highly sought after novels. With beautiful cover art created by artist Erica Just, this is a Collector's Edition to cherish.

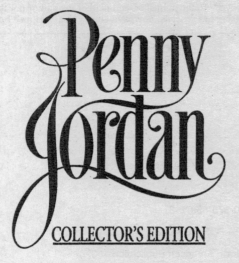

Penny Jordan

COLLECTOR'S EDITION

Desire for Revenge

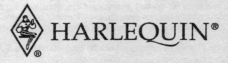

HARLEQUIN®

TORONTO • NEW YORK • LONDON
AMSTERDAM • PARIS • SYDNEY • HAMBURG
STOCKHOLM • ATHENS • TOKYO • MILAN • MADRID
PRAGUE • WARSAW • BUDAPEST • AUCKLAND

ISBN 0-373-83376-8

DESIRE FOR REVENGE

First North American Publication 1987.

ERICA JUST
cover illustrator for the
Penny Jordan Collector's Edition

Erica Just is an artist and illustrator working in various media, including watercolor, pen and ink, and textiles. Her studio is in Nottingham, England.

Her work is inspired by the natural forms, architecture and vibrant colors that she has experienced on her travels, most especially in Africa and India.

Erica has exhibited her work extensively in Great Britain and Europe and has works in private and public collections. As an illustrator she works for a number of companies and also lectures on textile design throughout the country.

CHAPTER ONE

'Look David, I think this has gone far enough
I. . .'

'I *want* you Sarah, and I always get what I
want, especially when what I want happens to be
a green-eyed witch with red hair and a body just
made for love, even though something tells me
that that body has never actually experienced the
total reality of a man's love.'

She felt trapped; half mesmerised by the deliberately soft monotone of his voice, and not even
the fact that they were in her office, within easy
screaming distance of her fellow employees, had
the power to make her feel fully safe. And
besides, what sort of executive would she be if
she let one mere man sexually intimidate her to
the extent where she was panicked into reacting
like a naïve teenager?

Gathering herself together, Sarah took a deep
breath and then said as calmly as she could,
'David we've been through all this before. You
might be a valuable asset to the company, but I
am not prepared to go to bed with you just so
that you will continue to use Leichner & Holland
as your publishers. And I'm sure that Steven
would back me up in this.'

Steven Holland was the owner of Leichner & Holland and it was he who had been responsible for promoting Sarah a year ago from being assistant editor to the status of fiction editor, with a special responsibility for the new avenue of fiction aimed at women, which they were pursuing. Sarah did not delude herself as to her abilities; she had been promoted as a result of something which had really been little more than a lucky fluke. She had been idly reading through a manuscript which James Richards, the chief fiction editor, had thrown on one side and had immediately been struck by the emotive way in which the story had been written. The name of the writer had been unknown to her, but she still found the novel powerfully compelling. She had been reading it one lunch hour over her coffee and sandwich when Steven had passed her on the way to his office. He had questioned her about what she was reading, and after being amused by her enthusiasm had said that since she was so enthusiastic about the work he might as well read it for himself.

Slightly to Sarah's surprise he had been as enthusiastic as she was herself, and the result was that she was now officially Fiction Editor (Female) for Leichner & Holland.

Of course her promotion had not been without problems. For one thing James Richards had objected strenuously to it, and Sarah had heard only the other day that he had actually now given in his notice. There had been a lot of talk about who might replace him, but as yet nothing official.

'I mean it Sarah. . .I want you and I mean to have you. . .'

'But not here I trust, David. . .' she managed to quip acidly. His remark about her virginity rankled and worse, made her feel acutely vulnerable. Sarah was no fool. She recognised very strongly in David Randal a very basic masculine drive to possess and subjugate the female sex. The fact that, as he had so correctly guessed, she was still a virgin made him all the more keen in his pursuit of her.

She watched him get up and leave her office, gnawing anxiously on her bottom lip. How he felt about the female sex came across very clearly to her in his books. Sarah did not like them at all. He wrote under a female pseudonym, and that in her opinion, was the only reason he managed to get away with some passages that were in effect little more than a lascivious description of female degradation. She had already expressed her doubts to Steven about David's latest manuscript, but it was an undeniable fact that the long historical novels he wrote, sold well. At the last group meeting of the editors responsible for the various types of books the firm published, James Richards had bitterly opposed her suggestion that they ceased publishing David's work. He had even accused her of wanting to cut David from their lists because she disliked him personally as a man, which had been a very difficult accusation to refute without revealing the truth.

Sarah had few illusions about either her own ability or the security of her position. If she once admitted that she could not handle sexual harassment from an author she could well soon find herself demoted. It was ridiculous that at the grand old age of twenty-five she should find herself in this position, but trying to make it plain to David Randal that she did not find him in the least attractive was like trying to build a snowman in the Sahara desert—a complete waste of time and effort.

She even suspected that he found her dislike of him a challenge. It was her virginity that attracted him the most, Sarah thought wryly, as she sat back in her chair. Without that she would simply be another passably attractive woman. How had he guessed? Perhaps it had something to do with the way she always recoiled from him whenever he came anywhere near her. . . She had disliked him even when she had had little to do with him, but now. . . She had heard it said that an experienced man could always tell when a woman was unawakened. Until now she had never really believed it.

She picked up her pen and toyed absently with it. The simplest answer would be for her to leave and find another job. . .but where would she find one as congenial as this? And one that paid as much. With her promotion had come a very useful pay rise. . . And very timely it had been, too, with Gran suddenly too feeble to look after herself, and Jane worrying herself sick about how she was going to cope with triplets under five, a husband, a rambling, half-modernised country vicarage, an assortment of pets, and Gran as well. Especially when the doctor had told them that because of the delusions she sometimes experienced, Gran needed to be watched for most of the time.

The extra money she was earning, plus the sale of Gran's small house, plus what Jane's husband, Ralph, could provide had meant that they were able to pay for Gran to stay in a really good residential home close enough to the Gloucestershire village where Jane and her family lived, for Jane to be able to visit once a week, and for Gran to join in all the family events. If she had to go back to working merely as a secretary—even in a really good job—she would not be able to make her contribution any more.

Tears blurred her eyes for a moment and she brushed them away impatiently. She so desperately wanted to do all she could to help Jane and Ralph. They had done so much for her. Jane had been twenty-one and newly engaged when their parents had been killed in a road accident; Sarah had been fourteen.

Ralph had not hesitated. Although he had just been on the point of leaving the firm he worked for and setting up in business on his own, he had said instantly that he and Jane would marry, and that Sarah would make her home with them.

Right through university Ralph had supported her, and it was only in this last year that he had realised his dream of starting up his own computer software business. Ralph was the complete antithesis of a man like David Randal. He was a devoted husband, a caring father. . .hardworking, good humoured. He had done so much for her. . . helping out now with the expense of caring for Gran was the least she could do.

So what was the answer? Sarah didn't really know.

'You look pensive. . . Problems?'

She looked up and smiled at the pretty, curly haired brunette standing in the doorway.

Rachel had taken over from her as assistant editor, having been Steven's secretary previously, and Sarah liked her very much.

'Not really,' Sarah lied. 'Does Steven want me for something?'

'Not as far as I know. It's lunch time and we have a date. . .remember?'

Lunch time already? Sarah sighed. How long had she been sitting there worrying about David?

'I see you've had a visit from one of our least favourite authors this morning,' Rachel commented, when Sarah got up to join her. 'Is he giving you problems?'

'No more than usual.' She pulled a wry face. 'You know what he's like.'

'Yeah! Personally I can't stand those aggressively sexual types. I don't know how his poor wife puts up with him. He's always got some woman going on the side, although they don't normally last long.'

They reached the lift and stopped talking as they got into it and descended to the ground floor.

'Heard the news about who's going to take over from James Richards?' Rachel asked as they stepped out into the gusty March wind. 'It's now official.'

'No. I haven't heard a thing.'

'Well, it's official now,' Rachel told her as they sat down in the small wine bar they patronised every Friday lunch time. 'Our new Editor in Chief is going to be no less than the great Joshua Howard, himself.'

'Joshua Howard!' Sarah was impressed. There could be few people in the journalistic or publishing world who would not be at the mention of his name. Although only in his early thirties he had a formidable reputation in the media world.

From being a foreign correspondent with *The Times* he had gone on to write several stunningly successful 'faction' novels based on some of the events he had covered during his years as a reporter.

To Sarah's knowledge at least one of them had been made into a film, and in view of all this it struck her as rather odd that such a famous and surely wealthy man should be content to take a job as editor with such a small, albeit prestigious, firm as Leichner & Holland.

'Of course, he isn't coming is as editor,' Rachel confided. 'I know you know that the firm's been having a few financial problems recently—the new Cartwright novel bombed for one thing, and the legal department is still trying to get back that advance we paid to Wayne Johnson.'

Sarah did know. The loss of the massive advance paid to Wayne Johnson the pop singer who had begun his meteoric career in the early sixties, had been a bitter blow to the firm. After over twelve months when the pop singer had still not produced a single chapter of his life story Steven had decided to try to get their advance back. That had been six months ago, and he was still not having success.

Steven had explained much of this to her when he had promoted her, telling her that he hoped a line of literature aimed specifically at the female end of the market might improve their fortunes, but new lines took time to develop and time, it seemed from what Rachel was telling her now, was something the firm simply did not have.

'Theoretically Joshua is just coming in as Editor in Chief,' she confided to Sarah, 'but in reality he's investing pretty heavily in the firm. Steven's still the owner and major shareholder of course; the Leichner line has pretty well died out, and neither of Steven's daughters want to come into the business, so I suspect that he intends grooming Joshua to take over from him when he eventually retires. You know that Joshua brought his first manuscript to Steven before he became well known?'

'Yes, I do.'

There could be few publishers as morally altruistic as her boss, Sarah reflected, recalling what he had told her, because he had recognised the book as a winner from the very first, but he had also known that his small publishing enterprise did not have the resources to promote the book as it needed to be promoted to ensure the world-wide success it deserved, and so he had recommended that Joshua try another publishing house, and had given the manuscript his own written commendation as well as giving Joshua an introduction to the American firm which had eventually published his work.

It was rather heartwarming to think that his kindness and generosity was now being repaid by Joshua Howard, and without having met him, Sarah felt herself warm to him.

'What's he like?' she asked Rachel curiously, 'I've never seen him.'

In response Rachel rolled her eyes heavenwards and sighed. 'Fantastic. . .and his smile is just so sexy that it made my bones melt.'

She saw Sarah's disbelieving expression, and grinned. 'Okay, don't believe me, but just wait

until you've seen him. Tall, dark, handsome. . .
Believe me he's got the lot and a body that—'

'Okay, okay! I think I get the picture. But does
Brian know that you—'

She broke off as Rachel grimaced and then
grinned. Brian was Rachel's fiancé, a pleasant,
tow-haired young man with a steady placid nature
that nicely balanced Rachel's more extrovert,
dizzy personality.

'Seriously, his personality seems to be just as
good as his looks,' Rachel told her. 'He's no
James Richards, but I don't think he's the type
to suffer fools gladly either. He doesn't seem to
hold any sexist views, but I don't see him as
the type to make any special allowances for us
females, just because we are females if you know
what I mean. . .'

With a sinking heart Sarah reflected that she
did. Steven, for instance, if she told him about
the problems she was having with David Randal,
would sympathise with her and try to find some
way of alleviating the problem, but to turn to
Steven meant going over the head of the Senior
Editor, which simply was not done. She had not
gone to James Richards for help or advice because
she knew he would only gloat over her dilemma,
and she had been hoping that the new person,
whoever that might be, might be someone more
understanding. The trouble was that the whole
problem was fraught with embarrassment and
difficulty. . . To explain it in full meant explaining

her own virginal state, which was something she was extremely reluctant to do. The easiest answer would be to get rid of her virginity, she reflected rather wryly, but at the moment that was easier said than done, since she had no current male friend. There had been opportunities at university, but she had found the work there so taxing and strenuous, and she had been so determined to repay Jane and Ralph for the financial support they were giving her, by getting a first-class degree, that there had been no time for boyfriends.

Afterwards there had been the initial struggle to get work; followed by the realisation that her degree did not really equip her for any particular job, meaning that she had had to work at night to get her secretarial qualifications. All in all there had been scant time for romantic involvements.

Despite her inexperience, Sarah was no fool. She knew quite well that it was the lure of her virginity as much as anything that attracted David to her. Without that. . . She also suspected it would not be much longer before he stopped asking and started demanding. She half suspected he would even go to the length of actually threatening her. He had hinted as much once or twice already. Even though she personally did not like the work he produced, it did earn money—money which the firm obviously badly needed at the present time. Once David started threatening to take his work elsewhere unless she gave in to him, what was she going to do? And Sarah knew it was only a matter of time before he *did* make that threat. She had already seriously damaged his ego, she knew that; and he was small-minded enough to want to make her pay for that.

'You're shivering. . .are you all right?'

Rachel's anxious query brought her back to reality.

'It's this icy wind,' she fibbed. 'London seems so cold at the moment.'

'Mmm. . . Spring's just round the corner, although you'd never guess it. Doing anything interesting this weekend?'

'I'm going down to my sister's. We're all going to a fancy dress ball—a local charity "do", and rather grand. . .' She pulled a slight face and Rachel laughed.

'You don't sound very enthusiastic. What are you going as?'

'I don't know. Jane's organising our costumes.'

In point of fact she wasn't particularly looking forward to the ball, but Jane had told her that the invitation had come from someone very influential locally, who was also a possible client for Ralph's business, and she had asked Sarah to support her and go with them.

'I'm scared out of my wits, that I might do the wrong thing,' she had confided over the 'phone, 'and I need my clever little sister by my side to give me confidence.'

In the face of that, there was little that Sarah

could do other than agree to go, but she wasn't looking forward to it.

For the rest of the afternoon she was quite busy. Steven made his announcement about James Richards' successor at half past four, and Sarah was slightly surprised to learn that Joshua Howard was actually coming into the office on Monday before he was due to begin working there. It seemed that James had demanded to be released from the usual notice period.

Sarah left the office at just gone five. Her suitcase was already packed and all she had to do was to get back to her small flat, shower and change, and then take a taxi to the station.

Ralph would pick her up in Gloucester. It was a routine which had been perfected over the eighteen months Sarah had worked for Leichner & Holland, and one which was now comfortably familiar.

By the time she arrived the triplets would be in bed, asleep, but they would be the first thing in the morning to wake her up—three boisterous and lovable four-year-olds whom Sarah secretly adored.

The three children—two boys and a girl—had been conceived by her sister after only a few months on a fertility drug when she had reached her early thirties with no sign of the child she and Ralph so desperately wanted. Jane had been over the moon, not at all fazed by the information that her doctor suspected that she was carrying more than one child, although up until the last moment no one had guessed the anticipated twins would be triplets. Her sister had a blissfully secure and happy life but no one could deserve it more than Jane. She and Ralph had both been so marvellous to her when Mum and Dad had been killed.

Her journey went smoothly. She found Ralph waiting for her when the train pulled in, his burly form instantly recognisable. He looked more like a farmer than a computer expert, Sarah reflected, returning his warm hug with enthusiasm.

'How is everyone?' she asked as they walked through the darkness to his waiting Range Rover.

'Fine. All dying to see you. Jane's been in a bit of a tizz this last week about the ball. She's managed to hire costumes for all of us and I've told her there's nothing to worry about.'

'I expect she's worried because she knows how important this contract is to you,' Sarah suggested, as she fastened her seat-belt.

'Mmm. . .I'm seeing Tom Merryweather tomorrow morning. I'm hoping he might give me a decision then. If he does, we'll push the boat out in style tomorrow night.'

They chatted in a casual fashion as Ralph drove along the familiar roads. Sarah had been brought up in this part of the world and knew it well. She also felt a deep sense of inner peace when she returned here and often wished it was possible for her to stay, but she had her living to earn, and at twenty-five she was far too young, or so Jane claimed, to settle for the stagnation of a country life.

Sarah was not deceived. Jane clucked as anxiously over her lack of menfriends as any mother hen, and Sarah knew that her sister was longing for the day she came home with a fiancé on her arm.

Her sister didn't wait for them to go inside to greet them. She came runing out of the house the moment the Range Rover turned into the Vicarage's overgrown drive. Ralph and Jane had only recently moved into their present house. Renovating and furnishing it was going to be a labour of love for both of them, and when they had finished Sarah knew they would have a home they could be justly proud of. At the moment, though, all was chaos. Ralph was doing most of the minor work himself, and since this took time, the back garden seemed constantly to resemble a builder's yard.

The Vicarage was early eighteenth century and had a substantial garden. There was even a small paddock for ponies for the children later if they required them.

'Come on inside, you must be shattered after the journey,' Jane commanded, hugging Sarah quickly as she got out of the Range Rover.

'Oh, yes indeed,' Sarah grinned. 'It took all of two hours or so and at my time of life. . .'

'Oh, you know what I mean. . . Come on I've

just made some fresh coffee. It seems ages since we last saw you. I want to hear everything that's been going on.'

'Well, if you two are going to gossip, I'm off to my study,' Ralph announced as he carried Sarah's cases into the large shabby hall. 'I'll take these up first for you, Sarah. You're in your usual room.'

'But this time you'll have your own bathroom,' Jane told her with a grin. 'Ralph finished converting that old dressing room off your bedroom last week. It looks fantastic.' She raised herself on tiptoe to kiss her husband's cheek, and watching them Sarah was conscious of a small piercing sensation of aloneness. What was wrong with her? She had never envied her sister her marital happiness before, why should she start doing so now?'

'Come on sit down and tell me what's making you look so miserable,' Jane commanded, when they were installed in the large, homely kitchen.

Modernising the kitchen had been Ralph's first priority when they moved in and he had done a marvellous job on it, Sarah reflected, studying the smooth richness of the dark oak kitchen cupboards with their antiqued tile worktops. From the original beams, which he had uncovered and retained, hung a various assortment of herbs and set into one wall was Jane's pride and joy— an ancient black-leaded fireplace complete with bread oven. On the wall in which the fireplace was set Ralph had exposed the original brick-work, and an assortment of brass pans now decorated it—all original antiques that Jane had cleverly found in local shops. A large, well-scrubbed and very old table took pride of place in the centre of the room, and it was on this that Jane placed their mugs of coffee as she pulled out chairs for them both, and passed a plate of home-made biscuits in Sarah's direction.

'I've tried a new recipe,' she commented, 'sugarfree so they're much better for the kids.'

'Speaking of which. . .'

'Oh, no you don't! I know when the subject's being changed. What's wrong, Sarah?' she asked dropping her bantering tone and looking seriously at her sister. 'Something is I know that much. Come on. . .give. . .'

Jane was much more to her than a mere sister, Sarah reflected as she slowly sipped her coffee. She had virtually brought her up from the age of fourteen, succouring her all through those difficult teenage years. It had been Jane who had listened to and answered all her questions about life and sex. Jane who had seen her through all her teenage traumas. She had never hidden anything from her sister, and it was impossible to do so now.

'Problems at work,' she said tersely. 'One of my writers is pushing me to have sex with him.'

'And the problem is that you don't want to. . . or that you do?' Jane asked frankly.

'I don't. . .' Sarah gave a tiny betraying

shudder. 'But he's putting a lot of pressure on me, and I suspect it won't be long before he actually threatens me. I can't turn to Steven for help—that would mean admitting that I can't handle the responsibility that goes with my job.'

'Mmm. . .I don't know about that.'

'The thing is this writer has guessed that I'm still a virgin, and that's why he's so determined to get me into bed.'

'Mmm. . .the old story of the male ego. Well, there is one simple solution.'

'Rid myself of said virginity,' Sarah said lightly. 'That had already occurred to me but it's not quite as easy as that, is it? After all, I can hardly go up to the first passably attractive male I see and say "would you mind making love to me?", can I?'

'No,' Jane laughed, agreeing with her. 'Is he married?' she asked.

'Very much so. I feel dreadfully sorry for his poor wife. He really is a loathsome specimen. The sort that makes your flesh creep. Oh, he's attractive enough I suppose in his way. . .but there's just something about him. . .'

'Mmm. I know what you mean, and I can understand your dilemma. Want me to look round for a suitable specimen of manhood for you?' she teased, bringing a lighter note to their conversation as Sarah grinned and replied threateningly, 'Just you try!'

They went on to talk about their grandmother,

who Jane told her had settled in extremely well at the home.

'I thought we might go and see her tomorrow afternoon. I've got to go into town to collect our costumes.' She made a wry face. 'I'm dreading this damned ball. It's the local social event of the year, you realise and we're extremely privileged to be invited.'

'I can tell that by your excitement,' Sarah responded solemnly, amusement dancing in her eyes. 'What are we going as?'

Jane smiled at her. 'Wait until you see our costumes. The do's being held at Merton Place, and since it was built at the height of the Georgian era, I've gone for very traditional Georgian outfits for all three of us. I had to go to Stratford to get them, I'll have you know—nowhere in Gloucester stocked anything that would do. They're theatrical costumes and very, very ornate. They're being sent by express delivery to the local station tonight, that's why we've got to go to town to pick them up tomorrow.'

'I can't wait to see Ralph dressed up as a Georgian dandy. . .' Sarah commented.

Jane gave a wicked giggle. 'I'm going to make him powder his hair but he doesn't know it yet! If it wasn't for the fact that we're being invited by one of Ralph's most important clients, I might be looking forward to it a little bit more.'

'You'll enjoy it when we're there,' Sarah consoled her sister and then, changing the subject, invited, 'Now tell me about my niece and nephews. . .'

'Come on, Auntie Sarah, wake up. . .'

Stubby fingers touched her eyelids, giggles erupting somewhere in the direction of her left ear. Someone was trying to tickle her ribs, and entering into the spirit of the game, she pretended she was still asleep, waiting until her three tormentors had given up trying to wake her before suddenly sitting up and grasping the nearest cuddly bundle and subjecting its ribs to the same torment so recently inflicted on her own.

The bundle in question just happened to be her niece, her helpless giggles and shrieks almost splitting Sarah's ears. The two boys, of course, had to join in the game, the three children only subdued when Jane marched into the bedroom carrying a mug of tea which she placed beside Sarah, at the same time, sternly telling her trio of offspring to take themselves off to their own rooms and get dressed.

'Little horrors,' she commented balefully when the triplets had finally departed, but Sarah wasn't deceived.

'And don't you just love them,' she agreed with a grin.

'Does it show that much? I suppose having had to wait so long for them. . .I must admit I'd just about given up hope.' She sighed and shook her head. 'Still there are some days when I do genuinely wonder why I ever bothered, and Louise is worse than the two boys put together. She can twist them and her father round her little finger.'

She sat down on the edge of Sarah's bed and said. 'What do you fancy doing this morning? I've done all the food shopping. The Vicar's wife is going to take charge of the kids tonight. Ralph will look after them while we're out this afternoon.'

'Well, since I'm feeling rather lazy this morning, how about my taking my niece and nephews for a short walk?'

'Great idea, if you're sure you don't mind,' Jane enthused. 'It will give me time to whip round with the vacuum before lunch. But be warned, don't let them persuade you to take them into the village, or you'll end up in the post office buying them sweets.

'Oh, by the way, Haughton House has been sold,' she added idly. 'I'm not sure who to. . .but I thought you'd like to know. You've always had a thing about the old place, haven't you?'

It was true, Sarah reflected half an hour later as she set off with a nephew firmly attached to either hand and her niece clinging firmly to the hand of one of her brothers. She had always been drawn to the beautiful Elizabethan manor house just outside the village.

It had been empty now for several months since the death of the last owner, and Sarah turned automatically in the direction of the footpath that led from the river, through a small wood, and then into the private grounds that went with the house.

At the boundary wall which separated the public footpath from the private, Sarah paused. The trees were not yet in full leaf and so she was able to see the house from where she stood. The sharp March sunlight turned the ancient brick-work to rose-gold, glinting here and there on mullioned windows. Apart from a couple of what appeared to be tradesmen's vans parked outside, there were no signs of activity.

Sighing faintly she responded to Jeremy's impatient tug on her left hand, and knew that as she obediently turned away from the house and back in the direction from which they had come that she had just said goodbye to a childhood dream.

As a teenager she had often come to this spot. There was a venerable oak tree several yards away, conveniently growing just by the boundary wall and in earlier years she had often hidden in its leafy branches simply daydreaming away a lazy summer's afternoon, imagining that she owned the house. . . In those far off days she had played many roles as chatelaine of the house; sometimes an Elizabethan maid of honour, hidden away down here from the Queen's wrath because she had caught the eye of one of her handsome courtiers; sometimes a secret Jacobite supporter, recklessly hiding one of the doomed Prince Charlie's wounded supporters; sometimes a be-muslined Regency girl waiting in trepidation to hand over her childhood home to the distant cousin who had inherited it from her father— whatever the setting for her daydreams might have been, they had always had the same conclusion; the male playing opposite her leading role as chatelaine inevitably fell in love with her and they lived happily ever after with the house as their home.

Sarah grimaced faintly. How long ago those days seemed now.

'Look, Auntie Sarah!' Paul tugged importantly on her right hand, speaking in a hushed whisper. 'There's a rabbit.'

Sure enough he was right, and all four of them paused for a second to admire the attractive little creature before he caught their scent and bolted for cover.

CHAPTER TWO

'Okay, are we ready?'

'As we're ever likely to be,' Sarah told her sister affectionately, as they hurried out to Jane's small Metro.

Her sister was a competent driver, and it didn't take them long to reach the nearby market town Jane used for most of her day-to-day shopping

'We'll go to the station first to collect the outfits and then get everything else.'

She parked neatly in the small station car park and Sarah went with her towards the tiny red-brick building.

The stationmaster greeted them with a smile, handing over the bulky parcels.

'Them'll be for that ball everyone's going to tonight,' he commented knowingly as Sarah took charge of them. 'A fine do it'll be, by all accounts. They say that the new owner of Haughton House will be there as well. A fine lot of work he's having done up at the place. . .there's a new swimming pool being put in—indoors, too—that'll cost him a fair penny.'

'Don't ever have any skeletons in your cupboard if you intend living in the country,' Jane groaned as she and Sarah stacked the boxes in the back of her car.

'What else do you need?' Sarah asked her as she tugged on her seat-belt.

'Nothing much, some nice biscuits for Mrs Arbuckle—I daredn't buy any before, the kids would have sneaked the lot. Some flowers for the house. I always like to have fresh ones for Sunday lunch.'

'Really?' Sarah kept her face straight as she teased. 'That's odd. . .I always thought Ralph was quite definitely a meat and two veg man!'

'Oh, for goodness sake you're as bad as the kids,' Jane complained but she was grinning, too, as they drove out of the car park.

As it was Saturday a small market was in progress and although they had some problems in parking, once they had done so, it didn't take them long to buy the bits and pieces Jane wanted.

'Fancy a cup of coffee before we go back?' She glanced at her watch. 'We've just about got time, and there's a rather nice new place that specialises in traditional afternoon teas.'

'Sounds good.'

The café was situated just off the small town square and had been attractively decorated in soft peach and grey. The cane chairs were painted white with peach seat covers, and despite the obvious bustle they were lucky enough to find an empty table, in the window.

'Mmm. . .this is nice,' Jane murmured as she

sat down. 'I daren't come in here with the brats, they'd cause too much chaos.'

They gave their order to a smiling waitress, and while Jane deliberated over a cream cake or a scone with jam and cream, complaining about the calorie intake of both, Sarah looked out of the window on to the busy street and the square.

A man walked across the road and into the square, his face in profile to her, his thick, black hair ruffled by the cool breeze. His skin looked tanned, his body tall and lean, with just a hint of breadth about the shoulders. Sarah's breath caught in her throat as he turned to check the traffic and she saw the intense sapphire blue of his eyes. As she looked she could almost see him as her Elizabethan gallant; her romantic Jacobite rebel; her reckless Regency rake. She blinked and swallowed hard and both the man and her inner visions of him were gone.

'Sarah, are you all right?'

She forced a shaky smile and nodded her head. 'Sorry, I was miles away. . .'

'Daydreaming,' Jane agreed wryly. 'I recognised all the signs, although to judge from the rapt expression on your face, it was a very special daydream. You're not holding out on me by any chance, are you?' she questioned severely. 'There isn't someone in your life I don't know anything about, is there?'

'Don't be silly. What on earth gave you that idea?'

'The look on your face,' Jane told her bluntly. 'You were looking as though Robert Redford had suddenly materialised in front of you.'

In spite of herself Sarah coloured faintly. The romantic daydreams of her teenage years were something she had long ago put behind her, and it was embarrassing to have them called to mind so strongly by the chance sighting of a strange man. She hadn't even seen him full face. . .but there had been something about him. . .quivers of sensation fluttered deep inside her, quickly banished when she realised the complete folly of the direction her thoughts were taking. It was both impossible and ridiculous to be so attracted to a man on mere sight.

'Come on, we'd better make a move,' Jane told her, consulting her watch again. 'I want the holy terrors bathed and in bed before Mrs Arbuckle arrives. Thank goodness Ralph has managed to install a separate bathroom for the guest room and for the nursery now, otherwise, we'd be queuing up for the same one from now until doomsday.'

'Read me another story, Auntie Sarah. . .' Sarah was in Louise's room, sitting beside the four-year-old's pretty Laura Ashley decorated bed.

'You've had two already,' she reminded her niece, hiding an appreciative grin at this bid to delay the moment of going to sleep a little further. . .

'Well then will you tell me another one tomorrow?'

'I tell you what, tomorrow night I'll tell you all about the ball.' Sarah offered.

Louise's eyes widened. 'Will there be princes there and princesses?' She was very much into fairy stories and Sarah repressed a small sigh for the vast gulf that lay between romance and reality.

She stood up and bent over the small figure of her niece to tuck the covers more securely around her, bending down to kiss her good night.

Ralph was reading to the boys, while Jane had her bath, and Mrs Arbuckle, the vicar's wife, was due in half an hour.

Checking that the night light was lit, Sarah let herself out of the room.

In her own room the dress she had unpacked and pressed on their return from town hung on the bathroom door. It was a gloriously rich Georgian costume in the most beautiful *eau de nil* silk, which opened over an underskirt of white satin embroidered with a complex design of silver flowers and leaves. At intervals the hem of the overskirt was caught up with white silk bows to reveal the satin underdress and the low neckline of the dress had a small pleated frill of white satin. The same fabric lined the sleeves from the elbows down, where they were caught up with ribbons. Sarah had no doubt that the dress was an exact replica of an original Georgian ballgown, and it was so supremely lovely that she felt she hardly dared to wear it.

In addition to the shoes provided to match the outfit there was a box containing combs and flowers attached to them for her hair, and several small patches with a brief handwritten note explaining where each one was to go and the precise meaning appertaining to each placement. Sarah raised her eyes a little over this, having had no idea that these adornments possessed their own special language. To complete the outfit there was even a fan in the same *eau de nil* silk as her gown.

Luckily her hair was long and naturally curly enough for her to pin it up in a small circlet of ringlets, which she coaxed to form by using her heated tongs. The effect, once she had pinned the flower combs in place, was surprisingly effective.

She took her time over her make-up, remembering that the fashion in the Georgian era was for pale skin, and having placed a small round patch just beneath her eye she sat back to study the whole effect. Even without powdering her hair it was surprising how different she looked. She and Jane had discussed doing this but had decided against it because of the mess involved.

She was just slipping her dress on when Jane came in. Her sister's eyebrows lifted in silent appreciation.

'Wow,' she exclaimed at last. 'You look fantastic. Turn round, I'll help you with the zip.'

'It doesn't have one,' Sarah pointed out wryly. 'Just one hundred million hooks and eyes.'

'An authentic touch we could well do without,' Jane grumbled as she fastened each of the tiny fastenings. 'There,' she exclaimed at last, 'now turn round.'

Sarah stared at her reflection in the mirror. It was unbelievable what a difference her costume made. She could have stepped out of a portrait of some Georgian lady.

'It's stunning,' Jane told her quietly. 'Absolutely stunning. . .'

Smiling, Sarah dropped her a brief curtsey, and unfurled her fan, looking demurely at her sister over the top of it. '*Merci*, My Lady,' she cooed dulcetly. 'You are too kind.'

Jane raised her eyes heavenwards. 'Okay, you can cut that out,' she instructed. 'Heavens, I'd better fly and get ready myself. I just came in to tell you that Mrs Arbuckle has arrived. Ralph is ready and downstairs entertaining her.'

'I'll come and give you a hand with your dress then, shall I?' Sarah offered.

Her sister's dress was a rich cobalt blue with gold embroidery, but slightly plainer than her own, and since her own hair was short, Jane had elected to wear with her outfit a period wig which she had also hired from the stage company.

Ralph's stare of amazement when they both went downstairs proved just how much their costumes transformed them. Mrs Arbuckle told them

half enviously that they looked wonderful and
although Ralph complained that the wig he was
wearing was making him itch, Sarah suspected
that her brother-in-law was enjoying the opportunity to dress up as much as they were themselves.

Because of the volume of the women's dresses
Ralph had decided that they might as well push
the boat out in style and had organised a chauf-
feur-driven limousine to take them to the ball.

'Much better than a coach and four,' Jane
exclaimed appreciatively as she sank down into
the comfortable leather seat. 'What do you
think, Sarah?'

Sarah agreed that Ralph had shown good sense
because between the two of them they took up
the entire length of the huge back seat leaving
Ralph to sit in front with the driver.

Their destination, the Georgian house where
the ball was being held, was only on the other side
of the village—a fifteen-minute drive at most.

For the occasion the driveway was illuminated
with Japanese flares in soft pastel colours, the
front of the house ablaze with lights. Several other
cars were disgorging their passengers when they
drew up, most of them garbed in Georgian
costume.

A liveried flunkey standing by the main door
requested their tickets and then ushered them
inside, where another liveried attendant indicated
the direction of the cloakrooms.

'The ballroom's on the second floor,' Jane

hissed to her sister as they followed several other women in the direction of the ladies' cloakroom.

Having checked that her wig wasn't in any danger of disgracing her, Jane suggested that they go upstairs.

Outside the doors to the ballroom Ralph was waiting for them, talking to another couple. His male companion was rather portly, and looked flushed beneath his heavy wig. He greeted Jane with a brief kiss on the cheek as did the woman with him.

'And this is Sarah, my sister-in-law,' Ralph introduced her. 'Tom and Veronica Merryweather. . . Veronica was partially responsible for organising this affair tonight.'

Veronica Merryweather was small and plump, wearing a gown that displayed her pretty shoulders. Sarah guessed shrewdly that the collar of diamonds she was wearing round her throat was genuine, and she also suspected from the slight tension she could feel emanating from her sister that Jane was a little on edge in her presence.

'I'm sorry, but we're going to have to desert you,' Veronica Merryweather apologised with a smile. 'I'm on the committee organising the ball. . .and I'm supposed to be on duty downstairs greeting the new arrivals.'

'See you in the bar later, eh, Ralph,' her husband suggested, clapping Ralph genially on the back, as he turned to follow his wife.

The ballroom was easily large enough to hold

the five hundred guests invited, and off it were
three other reception rooms which had been con-
verted into supper rooms for the purpose of the
ball, Jane explained to her sister, breaking off her
commentary to exclaim, 'Good heavens. . .look
over there. . .isn't that Lady Fentham? Over there
in the puce satin trimmed with some sort of fur.
No, there, Sarah.' She tugged her sister's arm
pointing her in the direction she wished her to
look, and all of a sudden Sarah froze. She could
see the woman Jane was talking about—but she
wasn't the one who held her interest. Just behind
her, but clearly discernible to Sarah, was the man
she had seen in the town square that afternoon.
It was true that now he was wearing a powdered
queue of hair, but there was no mistaking that
distinctly masculine profile, nor the intense blue
of those sapphire eyes. He turned his head and
for a moment it seemed as though he were looking
directly at her. For the first time in her life Sarah
knew what it meant when someone said their
heart missed a beat. Hers seemed to stop completely, the world tilting slowly and then equally
slowly righting itself again. She could feel the
colour crawling up under her skin, mirroring the
intense heat building up inside her. She felt both
light-headed enough to float and at the same time
almost unable to make any movement that might
disengage her attention from the man she was
watching.

'Sarah, come back. . .'

Reluctantly she looked away and met her sister's exasperated eyes.

'For goodness sake. . .stop worrying about work. You're here tonight to enjoy yourself— remember?'

It seemed impossible to Sarah that Jane had not realised the real reason for her inattention. She heard herself make some absent remark about Lady Fentham's outfit, and she listened while Jane pointed out other local dignitaries to her. Some of them she recognised from her teens. . . others were people Jane and Ralph had got to know since Ralph had been in business on his own.

Several people came up to talk to them; more than one commented on the attractiveness of her own and Jane's costumes, and Sarah had to admit that they were vastly superior to those most of the guests were wearing.

When she made a comment to this effect Jane pulled a slight face. 'I know it seems trivial and petty, but now that Ralph's in business on his own, we do have to keep up appearances. Nothing inspires confidence in the business world quite as much as an outward show of success. . .but our dresses are lovely, aren't they?' She smoothed an appreciative hand over her own skirt. 'Worth every extra penny it cost to hire them. It was Veronica who tipped me off about where to get them. She's quite an old hand at these charity dos.

'Where on earth is Ralph?' she added frowning

slightly. 'He's been gone ages. He's probably talking business somewhere in the bar!'

'He's coming now,' Sarah told her, having spotted her brother-in-law making his way towards them.

'Come on with me, you two,' he instructed, 'we've got some celebrating to do.' He was standing closer to Sarah than to Jane, and slipped his arm round Sarah's waist, hugging her to him and kissed her on the cheek.

Without knowing why she did so Sarah looked across the room. Her heart started to thud with slow heavy beats as sapphire eyes engaged her own. It was as though a message passed between them; hers saying, 'His kiss means nothing,' and his replying, 'No. I know. . .but mine will.'

She shuddered, only half listening as Ralph enquired anxiously. 'Are you cold? You shivered. . .'

Sarah shook her head, her heart beating so fast, she felt as though it might choke her. Ralph had his other arm round Jane now and he was propelling them both towards the door to one of the supper rooms. Sarah felt as though she didn't want to move; as though she would give anything not to break that contact so recently and so powerfully established.

The sensation she was experiencing was like nothing she had known before; a sexual magnetism so strong that it seemed almost other-worldly. It was as though a rapport had been established that was so strong and direct that no words were necessary. Unwillingly she let Ralph urge her away, amazed that neither he nor Jane seemed to be aware of what was happening to her. She had felt the power of that concentrated sapphire gaze so intensely that she couldn't believe that no one else was aware of it.

'This way,' Ralph directed once they were in the supper room, guiding them in the direction of a table at which the Merryweathers sat.

Tom Merryweather stood up as they approached, pulling out chairs first for Jane and then for Sarah.

A bottle of champagne in an ice bucket stood beside the table, five tulip-shaped glasses waiting to receive the bubbly liquid.

'Well, Ralph?' Tom queried jovially. 'Have you told them the good news yet?'

'I thought I'd better get Jane sitting down first,' Ralph grinned. 'Tom's just told me that we've got the contract for the software program for his new computer.'

After the buzz of excitement had died down, Tom Merryweather signalled to a hovering waiter to pour the champagne, getting to his feet to toast the success of Ralph's business.

Sarah was thrilled for her sister and brother-in-law, knowing from what they had told her, what a difference this important contract would make to their lives, and Ralph had also confided that where Tom Merryweather led, others were likely to follow.

The bottle of champagne Tom ordered was a magnum, and by the time Ralph was pressing her third glass of champagne on her, Sarah was feeling decidedly light-headed. She had little head for alcohol at the best of times and the euphoria of hearing about Ralph's success, combined with the dizzying sense of instantaneous recognition that had flashed between her and the man she had seen in the town square that afternoon seemed to have completely removed her normal reticence. She found herself laughing as easily as Jane at Tom Merryweather's teasing jokes, and even flirting rather mildly with the older man when he praised her outfit.

Veronica Merryweather was quieter than her husband; a pretty rather than elegant woman, who Sarah suspected was a perfect foil for her more exuberant mate. There was no doubt that they were an extremely happily married couple. They had two daughters, Sarah learned, as she drank her champagne, both married and with children of their own now, and it had been as a direct result of one of their grandchildren desperately needing a very difficult heart operation as a baby which had led to Veronica's heavy involvement in charity fund raising.

Despite the muzzy sensation brought on by the unaccustomed champagne Sarah could see that through Ralph's business connections with Tom, her sister was also likely to become involved in working alongside Veronica in her fund raising work. It was a role that would ideally suit her sister, who was already beginning to wonder what she would do with her time once the triplets were at school. Jane had a tremendous flair for organisation and Sarah was pleased to see that this gift would find a proper outlet.

They heard the small dance combo striking up a waltz, and across the table Veronica grinned at her husband and instructed, 'We're going to dance this waltz, even if it's the only time I manage to get you on the floor tonight—they played it for us at our reception when we were married,' she explained to everyone else.

'And I asked them to play it for us tonight,' Tom told her with a corresponding grin.

'What do you think of them?' Jane asked Sarah when they had gone.

'I like them. He seems very down to earth, shrewd, but completely honest, not the sort of man it would be easy to fool, or deceive.'

'No, he's got no time for what he calls "posers",' Ralph told her. 'A few of the old brigade locally don't care for him—but I've always found him pleasant enough. He's apt to call a spade a spade, and he's come on in life the hard way. He'll have no truck with any pretence but he's exceptionally kind-hearted—and not because he's one of these self-made millionaires who's out to buy himself a peerage, either.'

'You must be thrilled to bits about the contract,' Sarah enthused to Ralph. 'It will make all the difference to the business. The pair of you should be out celebrating alone tonight without having me tagging along.'

'Oh, we can celebrate in private later on.'

Ralph grinned, laughing when Jane blushed slightly and said reprovingly, 'Ralph. . .'

'But if you'll excuse us, Sarah, I would like to dance with my wife.'

'Dancing. . .is that what you call it,' Jane groaned, but nevertheless she stood up, pausing only to say to Sarah, 'Are you sure you don't mind?'

'Don't be silly. Off you go.'

Slowly sipping what was left of her champagne Sarah sat back in her chair and studied her surroundings. Apart from a disconcerting tendency to sway rather unnervingly whenever she chanced to move her head too quickly, she could find nothing to criticise in the very traditional Adam décor of the room she was in. The walls had panels in the same *eau de nil* as her gown, a similar colour contrasted with a soft butter yellow used on the intricately plasterworked ceiling, with the plasterwork itself picked out in white and embellished with gold.

At one end of the room was an Adam fireplace over which hung a giltwood mirror. Several portraits ornamented the rooms, and Sarah was studying one several yards away, a mother and daughter study very much in the style of Lely, wondering if it was genuine, when a voice against her ear made her jump and clutch wildly at the stem of her champagne glass, her eyes swivelling from the picture to those of the man bending over her.

'She was reputed to be one of Charles II's many mistresses,' he murmured dulcetly. 'That was how the family got this land. Lely in his time had a reputation for being the portraitist of the "Royal Whores".'

'So it is genuine?'

The last thing she wanted to do was to talk about their hostess's art collection. Her heart was thumping so loudly it seemed impossible that she was actually able to carry on a normal conversation. How she managed to be so deeply engrossed in staring at the portrait that she had not heard him approach, especially since she had had every sense attuned for him ever since she had seen him in the ballroom, she had no idea.

At close quarters his eyes were even more darkly blue than she had realised, fringed with thick black lashes, his tanned skin, and slightly mocking expression somehow making him look far more at ease in his costume than any of the other men present.

'I shouldn't think so. . .but it's a passable enough copy. The original was probably sold years ago. Would you care for another drink?'

Sarah grimaced ruefully into her empty glass.

'I don't think I'd better,' she admitted frankly, 'I have absolutely no head for chamgagne and that was my third glass. At the moment I doubt if I could so much as walk in a straight line from here to the ballroom!'

'Why don't we give it a try?'

Before she knew what was happening he was gently tugging her out of her seat, sliding his hands to her waist to support her as she stood somewhat shakily. As he bent to steady her his jaw was on a level with her mouth and she ached to touch her lips to its hard firmness. A sensation of mild shock quivered through her, its intensity muted by the champagne she had consumed, and as he guided her towards the ballroom, it suddenly struck Sarah that here was the ideal candidate with whom to rid herself of the tiresome burden of her virginity. Every female sense she possessed told her that this man would be a lover whose touch, once experienced, would never be forgotten, and above and beyond that there was something about him that reached out to her on the most primitive and intense level of her being. She wanted to make love with him, she acknowledged inwardly; and the admission brought her no shame or shock, merely a sense of rightness. She trembled, and although she knew he must have felt her physical reaction, unlike Ralph he did not ask her if she was cold, merely lifting one eyebrow and smiling down at her rather quizzically.

'Before I steal you away, I take it the gentleman I saw you with earlier has no prior claim on you that I should know about?'

She liked that in him, Sarah thought muzzily; that he should so clearly and yet so inoffensively make his desire for her plain, and yet at the same time want to make sure that she was free to reciprocate that desire.

'None at all,' she assured him. 'Ralph is my brother-in-law.'

'Unfortunate man.' He drawled the words softly, releasing her waist with his right hand to hold her arm, his thumb stroking softly over the vulnerable underside of her skin where the sleeve fell away from her elbow. While she was still shuddering with delicate pleasure he bent his head and caressed the inner curve of her elbow with his mouth before lifting her hand to his lips and slowly kissing the tip of each finger.

A weird swooning sensation turned her blood hot and sluggish in her veins, a pleasure so intense and all-consuming enveloping her that she moved automatically into his arms, clinging to his shoulders as her body trembled its age-old message against his.

'I want to make love to you.'

The words fell gently against her skin as he murmured them into her ear.

In an almost dreamlike sequence Sarah heard herself replying huskily, 'I want it too. . .'

It was something she had never envisaged happening to herself; this instantaneous rapport; this surge of sheer physical desire so strong that nothing could make itself heard above it. Already she could imagine herself in his arms, touching his skin, caressing him as he caressed her in turn; and as her body trembled beneath the erotic images her mind was conjuring up, Sarah knew that her desire to give herself to this man had little or nothing to do with losing her virginity, but she dismissed that knowledge, banishing it to the furthermost recess of her mind, knowing that to admit it was to open herself to a danger she was not yet ready to face.

CHAPTER THREE

THEY danced, once. . . .twice. . . .on the surface, neither of them in a hurry to precipitate what they both knew would be the culmination of the evening, but beneath it. . . Every time his body brushed hers in the movement of the dance Sarah was conscious of heightening excitement. . .of intense hunger, of an ache that tightened to a refined form of torture, and she knew that he felt it, too.

She had long ago forgotten about Ralph and Jane, and when the grandfather clock in one of the ante-rooms finally struck twelve she looked questioningly at her partner.

'Yes,' he murmured softly. 'I think it's time we left. . .I have a cottage a few miles away.'

The prosaic words held a question, and Sarah nodded her head and whispered shakily, 'Take me there.'

She saw the smile curl his mouth and the rather whimsical expression in his eyes. 'Just like that? You're very trusting. We don't even know one another's names. . .'

Without knowing why she did it, Sarah reached up and pressed her fingers to his mouth. It felt hot against her skin, his lips parting to moistly caress her fingertips. Rivulets of sensation spread through her body, like darts of lightning.

'Tonight's a fairytale night,' she told him softly. 'A gift from a fairy godmother. . .let's keep it like that.'

She didn't want to talk to him. . .she didn't want him to take on a more real form for her than the one he already had. Already some part of her knew that she must preserve something of herself from him for her own safety. It was easier like this. . .easier to pretend that this was all part of a dream, a fantasy come to life. Instinct told her that she could trust him, that he was no sadist, no violent psychopath who would do her any physical harm. The pull of her senses towards him was so strong that she dared not let there be anything more than that between them.

He was a lover sent to her as a gift by fate, or so her champagne-bemused brain told her, and she didn't want to analyse the situation any further than that.

It never even occurred to her to tell Ralph and Jane that she was leaving. She had no wrap with her, and it was the simplest thing in the world to let him lead her downstairs and out into the night; for them to stop beside a sleek Porsche sports car, which he unlocked and then carefully tucked her into.

She felt too dreamily hazy even to fasten her seat-belt, letting him do it for her, breathing in the male scent of his skin. He took off the periwig he had been wearing as part of his costume and tossed it into the back of the car before starting the engine. His hair, thick and black, lay close to his skull, making her ache to touch it; to feel its softness beneath her fingertips. She closed her eyes as he set the car in motion.

His cottage was a middle one in a short row of what had once been estate workers' homes, down by the river. The headlights from the Porsche as he swung it to a halt picked out the stone façade with its white-painted trellis on which a clematis was just beginning to put out new spring tendrils of green.

As he switched off the engine silence enveloped them. This was the moment when she ought to be having second thoughts Sarah realised, but instead she was wrapped in a blanket of euphoria, a feeling of such intense happiness spreading through her that she herself could hardly believe it was real. She seemed to have been freed of all moral and mental restraints; free to follow her emotions and her desires in a way that was totally unfamiliar.

It was only as he helped her out of the car that her companion said rawly, 'Do you realise that we haven't even exchanged first names yet?'

Sarah smiled at him. She felt no fear; no hesitation, only an intense sense of rightness.

'Is that a gentlemanly way of telling me that you're having second thoughts?'

They were standing under the small porch by

the front door and he turned her towards him, his hands cupping her face so tightly that she could feel the faint callouses on his fingers imprinting against her face.

'No way,' he told her huskily. 'I wanted you the moment I set eyes on you.'

'Even without knowing my name?'

It was the first time Sarah had ever played such a teasing flirtations game and the look that darkened his eyes was as heady to her senses as the earlier champagne had been.

'What's in a name?' He muttered it against her skin, caressing her jawline with his lips, smoothing a stray ringlet behind her ear. 'I only know that from the first moment I saw you, I knew I wanted you in my arms...in my bed,' he told her fiercely, adding on a lighter note, 'What is your name?'

'Sarah,' she told him promptly, not vouchsafing her surname; it didn't seem necessary.

'Mine's Joss,' he responded, smothering her response with the fierce, heated pressure of his mouth.

His kiss obliterated the last remnants of her other saner self. She clung to him, welcoming the taut contraction of his muscles as she slid her hands beneath his jacket and clutched his shoulders. Her own body seemed to be a boneless, fluid entity incomplete without the hard strength of his against it. Her lips parted readily to welcome the heat of his tongue. His hand stroked up from her waist, moulding her breast, caressing her convulsively, and immediately she ached to be rid of the barriers of her clothes. She wanted his hands on her body...his skin, his mouth... against her own.

When his mouth abruptly left hers, she felt bereft; almost abandoned. Her lungs ached from the cold night air and she was shivering.

Joss was as affected as she was herself, fighting to control his own ragged breathing. His voice was deep and raw as he muttered, 'For God's sake, what are you doing to me? You've got me in such a state I could almost take you right here. We'd better go inside while I'm still capable of doing anything that doesn't involve having you in my arms.'

He turned away from her to unlock the door, and then preceded her inside to switch on a light.

Sarah followed him, blinking in the light which illuminated the tiny sitting room. She noticed rather absently that the small room had been attractively renovated, and that it was pleasantly furnished, but her mind was not on the décor. A flight of open stairs led up from the sitting room and involuntarily her eyes followed it.

She managed to drag her attention away, feeling the colour crawl up over her skin as she saw that Joss was watching her, the same hungry burning need she could feel eating away at her, openly displayed in his eyes. She felt oddly light-headed, and moved automatically towards him.

He held out his hands, not to take hold of her, but to hold her off. For a moment rejection and pain sliced through her.

'Don't look at me like that,' he demanded thickly. 'If I touch you now, I'll end up making love to you here where we're standing like a raw teenager. Who are you, lovely Sarah?' he whispered huskily. 'What magic do you possess to make me feel this way?'

Slowly Sarah reached out and touched her fingers to his lips, her body tensing under their warmth, her senses relaying to her the knowledge that he was as affected as she was herself by that brief contact.

'No questions. Tonight is special,' she told him softly. 'If there is any magic, it's in the fact that tonight we've found one another. Let's not spoil it by questioning why.'

She saw his eyes narrow faintly, and tensed herself, unwilling to question too deeply her desire to keep her image of him as a complete stranger. It was because she didn't want to be disillusioned that she didn't want to know more about him, she told herself defensively, but somewhere deep inside her part of her knew better. It was fear that urged the secrecy on her; fear that the more she knew about this man the more she would want to know.

Joss took her hand and led her towards the stairs, pausing there to demand rawly, 'Are you sure this is what you want, Sarah?'

She liked that in him; that he was man enough to give her the chance to back out if she wished.

'More than anything I've ever wanted in my entire life,' she told him and it was no less than the truth.

The smile he gave her was whimsical, edged with faint self-mockery. 'You might not believe this. . .but this is the first time anything like this has ever happened to me,' he told her softly. 'Just for the record, I don't make a habit of making love to strange ladies, no matter how beautiful they might be.'

'I'm glad that in my case you're prepared to make an exception.' Sarah said it demurely, but there was nothing demure about the way she looked at him, letting him lead her up the narrow flight of stairs.

Two doors opened off the small landing, and Joss turned the handle of the first of them, flicking a switch that snapped on a bedside lamp.

The room was furnished in soft greys and blues; the walls papered in a fabric that looked vaguely Sandersonish. A matching bedspread covered the bed, a soft blue-grey carpet underfoot.

Somehow, the room did not match the man; neither had the room downstairs Sarah thought reflectively. Intuitively she suspected that this was not his permanent home, and then she closed her mind to such thoughts because Joss was removing the satin coat that was part of his costume and coming towards her.

It struck her then vaguely that Ralph and Jane might be missing her, but she dismissed the knowledge. She was an adult, capable of making her own decisions in life. Perhaps after their discussion, Jane might even guess what she was doing. But was it purely because of David that she was here tonight with Joss? Sarah knew it was not; even without David she would still be here. Tonight was something she was embracing for herself, because intuitively she knew that not to do so was to deprive herself in a way she would regret for the rest of her life.

Even without the wig which had been part of his costume, standing there with the falls of lace at his wrists startlingly white against the tan of his skin, slowly opening the laces that fastened the front of his shirt, he still looked very much as though he had actually come from that bygone age.

'Sarah.' He said her name unsteadily, his voice thick and hot. A convulsive wave of desire clutched at her stomach, her heart pounding at a dizzying speed. Ridiculous to have reached the grand old age of twenty-five and never experienced these sensations before.

He was standing completely motionless looking at her and beneath the low, tightly cut neckline of her costume Sarah felt her breasts swell and ache. She looked at his hands, imagining them against her skin, bemused by the unexpected flood of heat storming over her. She lifted her eyes from Joss's hands to his face. A tiny nerve flickered betrayingly beneath his skin, his eyes reflecting the heat she could feel beating through her own body.

She watched, completely unable to move as he stripped off his shirt with economical, almost savage movements that left his torso bare, his skin gleaming warm gold in the muted light from the lamp. His shoulders were broad with hard muscles, his chest deep, narrowing towards his waist.

Her attention concentrated totally upon him Sarah marvelled at the male perfection of his body, a need to caress and explore it exploding achingly inside her. She took a step towards him, stumbling a little; she heard him curse as he fumbled with the fastenings of his satin knee breeches. The light caught the silken play of the muscles beneath his skin, shadowing the darker areas of his body where fine silky hair covered his flesh.

He sat down on the bed to remove his shoes and stockings and for the first time a quiver of apprehension touched Sarah's senses as she realised the total masculinity of him. He stood up, tall, much taller than she was herself, very little of his physique concealed by the briefs he still wore.

'Come here. . .'

The words, spoken softly with a husky, raw

note of need, banished her apprehension and she went to him, smiling a little wryly at the contrast they must present—Joss practically nude, herself still clothed in her voluminous skirts. And then she remembered the multitude of tiny fastenings that secured it.

Turning her back to him she said lightly, 'I'm afraid I'm going to need some help getting this off.'

She shuddered as she felt his fingers touch her skin, pushing aside her hair. And then his mouth touched the vulnerable spot at the back of her neck and tiny shivers of delight rippled through every tiny nerve ending in her body.

With a maddening lack of haste, or so it seemed, Joss unfastened each tiny hook and eye, pausing to caress each inch of skin he revealed with the heat of his mouth.

The sensation of the fabric gradually giving way under his fingers alternating with the caressing warmth of his mouth against her body was the most erotic thing she had ever experienced.

When he reached her waist, the top of her dress fell away, revealing the full curves of her breasts and, as his hands slid round her body to cup them, Sarah arched convulsively back against him, sighing her pleasure in the delight the slow movement of his fingers against her nipples was arousing within her.

'Sarah!' She heard the urgency in his voice as

he muttered her name against her ear, her eyes opening and widening in sudden shock as she caught sight of their reflections in a mirror on the opposite wall.

In the shadowy half light the picture they presented was one of erotic intimacy; Joss's hands dark against her pale breasts, their unceasing movement and her body's response to it bringing to life within her a pagan physical desire she had never thought to know. Her body arched back against Joss. His dark head bent to her shoulder, and she shuddered beneath the pressure of his teeth against her sensitive skin, aching to reach out and touch him, wanting to feel the heat of his body, which was burning against her again, envelop every part of her.

His hands dropped from her breasts to her waist, his head lifting as he, too, studied their reflections. She looked. . .wanton, Sarah thought, searching for the right word to describe to herself the physical sexuality of her own appearance. Her hair was tumbling on to her shoulders, her breasts full, her nipples hard and darkly coloured. Even the way she was leaning back against Joss was suggestive of a careless abandonment. . .

Joss made a sound deep in his throat, something between a purr and a groan, and then he turned her into his arms, kissing her with a fierce pressure, his fingers moving swiftly over the remaining fastenings on her dress. She felt it fall free of her body, and drew away from his kiss to step free of it.

The simple act of doing so seemed to unleash something wild and elemental in Joss. He sat down on the bed, pulling her on to his lap, his mouth hot on the tiny pulse that danced at the base of her throat. Beneath the pressure of it she arched back against his arm, stifling the small sob of tormented pleasure that rose to her lips as she felt the heat of Joss's mouth against her breast. This was no tentative, explorative lover's caress, she acknowledged mutely, opening her eyes to gaze down at the darkness of his hair against her breasts as his mouth fastened over her swollen nipple and sucked fiercely on the tender skin.

Wave after wave of a pleasure as fierce as sheet lightning enveloped her body. . .her fingers clutched wildly at Joss's shoulder as the weight of his head against her breasts arched her further back over his arm. She could feel the maddened thud of his heartbeat against her body, the soft moans of delight she had been subduing in her throat exploding into a sharp cry as she felt the tormenting graze of his teeth against her skin.

When he released her breast he was breathing heavily, his free hand possessing the moist, aroused flesh so recently deserted by his mouth, the skilled movement of his thumb and finger against the aching peak of her breast making Sarah catch her breath and moan a husky plea to

be released from the torment he was inflicting
upon her.

'Sarah, Sarah, feel what you do to me.' He
muttered the words with fierce half incoherency
into her throat, tumbling her off his lap and on
to the bed, joining her there, to pull her into his
arms and hold her against the fierce throbbing of
his body.

Instinctively Sarah reached out to touch him,
tormented by the barrier of his briefs, impeding
the impatient stroke of her fingers along the dark
hair line of his body, only dimly registering his
impassioned shudder against her, until he said
thickly, 'No. . .no. . .not yet. . .I want to enjoy
every inch of you. . .I want this to be a night
neither of us will ever forget. . .'

He had already achieved that, Sarah thought
achingly, instinctively pressing her body against
his as he removed her fingers from his flat
stomach.

Her low moan of deprivation was entirely
involuntary, stilling the movements of his body,
and eventually her own, as Sarah opened tightly
closed eyes to find him watching her with an
intensity that blazed like fox fire from his eyes.

'From the moment I set eyes on you, I wanted
to see you like this,' he told her thickly. 'Your
eyes wild with wanting. . .your body open and
aching for mine.' His mouth touched her lips,
silencing the protest she was going to make and
it was impossible to resist the temptation to slide

her fingers into his hair, to mould the hard bones of his skull and let herself be submerged in the endless depths of pleasure he was offering her.

His mouth stroked her throat, lightly, caressingly, following the path of his hands, and as though a completely different person had taken over her body, Sarah arched and twisted meltingly beneath the skilled commands of his hands. His mouth touched her breast, where her nipple still ached from his earlier caresses. His tongue touched the sensitive flesh, lightly, rhythmically, tormentingly, until she cried out his name and slid her hands to his shoulders, arching her body upwards and shuddering in frantic pleasure as she felt his response to her need and totally abandoned herself to the fierce tug of his mouth against her breast.

She was so enraptured by the sensations he was arousing that it was several seconds before she realised that his hands were still caressing her body, stroking delicately along her inner thighs.

A warm heat built up inside her, the restless, eager movements of her body causing him to release her breast and mutter thickly against her ear.

'You're so damn responsive, you're making it impossible for me to hold on to any self-control.' He moved against her as he spoke and she could feel the truth of what he was saying in the fierce thrust of his body against her own.

A wave of desire and need so strong that it

overwhelmed everything else surged through her. Nipping him sharply with her teeth and feeling the convulsive clenching of his shoulder muscles beneath her mouth Sarah placed her lips against his ear.

Everything that she had lived by—had been before tonight was gone—as though she had been re-born a completely new person. With an openness the old Sarah could never have displayed, she whispered, 'I want you to make love to me. . .I want to feel you all around me. . .inside me. I want to. . .'

She let the words die beneath his mouth, revelling in the fierce masculine domination of his kiss. She felt him move while he was still kissing her and then sighed against his mouth her pleasure in the rough heaviness of his thighs against her own, their weight parting hers and making her shudder with awareness of the unfettered maleness of him against her.

'Sarah. . .lovely. . .lovely Sarah.' He was moaning her name like a litany against her skin, his hands fiercely possessive as they touched every part of her, his mouth hot as she felt the control slip from him as his body imposed upon them both demands as old as time.

His hand touched the moist centre of her body and she felt a leap of pleasure and anticipation. He touched her again, stroking and caressing and she moaned a faint protest at this further torment, a wild fever of urgency suddenly consuming her,

her hands caressing his body as freely as he had caressed hers, her senses revelling in the unmistakable surge of desire that flooded through him as she touched him intimately, her mouth registering the fierce beat of the pulse at the base of his throat as he moaned and arched beneath her touch, protesting at her feminine dominance and yet unable to resist submitting to the pleasure of it.

'Sarah.' She felt the shuddering tension that racked his body as he pulled away from her, and looked down into her face. There was something in his eyes that puzzled her; made her feel faintly wary and tense.

'What is it?' Her mouth had gone dry, tension flaring along her nerve paths.

'Just this.' He moved and his body entered hers with piercing sweetness. She held her breath, her eyes widening with the unexpectedly sweet shock of just what pleasure could be and heard him saying thickly. 'That's what I wanted to see. That you feel what I feel; that I'm not alone in feeling what I do.'

He moved again and she felt the slow, building thrust of his body within her own, her body automatically making him welcome, arching into the sensation of him moving within her, her hips lifting, her legs locking around his body.

She heard him moan her name as his body started to shudder with fierce pleasure, his mouth searching for and finding her own, the abrasive pressure of his chest against her breasts heightening the intense state of rapture. Dimly she was aware of some far-off, lancing pain, but the need driving her was all powerful, and even as she registered Joss's shocked recoil she was clinging fiercely to him, her body urging his to finish that which it had begun; to appease the need for fulfilment possessing them both and to give her the indescribable satisfaction of those spasms of pleasure which made her wrench her mouth from his to cry out in wonder that there could be such a sensation and then to murmur her delight at the knowledge that he, too, had touched those same heights.

As she gradually floated down from the clouds, a sleepiness she couldn't fight off engulfed her. Dimly she was aware of Joss calling her name, urgently, even impatiently, but she was too sleepy to respond. . . It was like floating downwards on the thickest and softest of down feathers. . .far too delicious to resist. . .

Sarah opened her eyes muzzily. She was having the strangest dream. She was a child again, sharing Jane's bed, as she had often done when she had suffered from childish nightmares. Jane's arm had been wrapped comfortingly round her. Sarah blinked and tensed as the dream became reality. There was an arm wrapped around her but it certainly wasn't Jane's!

With an appalling clarity she remembered everything that had happened. The lamp was still on and by its illumination she could see Joss's sleeping features.

Joss! She swallowed painfully. What on earth had she done? Biting her lip she remembered the questioning sharpness in his voice just before she had fallen asleep. He had known that she was a virgin. . . Dear heavens, she had to leave before he woke up. How on earth had she ever behaved in such a rash and totally alien way?

She moved experimentally and, holding her breath, managed to wriggle safely away from her sleeping companion without waking him. As she shivered in the cold of the room she became conscious of aches and sensations in her body that were wholly unfamiliar. Dark colour crept up under her skin as she visualised the events of the evening. Hurriedly she pulled on her clothes, trying not to make any noise. By turning her dress back to front she managed to secure all the lower fastenings, and with a struggle managed to secure enough of the upper ones to at least make herself look decent.

She had no idea what time it was, and daredn't risk waking Joss by looking for his watch, but it was still dark outside. As she finished dressing with feverish haste and then hurried to the bedroom door, she saw Joss stir, frowning deeply in his sleep. She held her breath until his movements stilled again, dreading his waking. It was best this way, she told herself as she opened the door and hurried downstairs. What had happened between them was already taking on a dreamlike quality. That it had not been a dream she was in no doubt about, but it was something so outside her normal experience of life and it seemed safer to hide it away completely. Even now she could hardly bear to think about the strength of the feelings he had aroused within her. As she let herself out into the darkened street, she shivered in the cold pre-dawn breeze. Thank God the cottage was within walking distance of Jane and Ralph's, although God alone knew what Jane was going to say when she got back.

There were no lights on in her sister's house, and no one stirred as she used her key to let herself in.

In her bedroom she undressed and then slid into bed without showering, not wanting to disturb anyone.

Even now she could scarcely believe what had happened. That she and a man who was a complete stranger had been lovers in the most intimate and passionate sense of the word. A rather wry smile curled her mouth as she lay in bed. At least now she would not have any more problems with David Randal. She almost laughed as she remembered Jane's advice to her to rid herself of her virginity. Then she had never imagined herself doing so, and certainly not in such a bizzare and out of character manner.

CHAPTER FOUR

'COME on, sleepyhead, wake up.'

Jane's familiar voice pierced through the clouds of sleep engulfing her, and Sarah frowned. There was something wrong about where she was, something missing. . . She flushed brilliantly as she realised what, or rather who it was, a fact which did not escape her sister's alert attention.

'Well,' Jane asked wryly, 'and where did you get to last night, or is it a state secret?'

'Only sort of.' Sarah sat up in bed, grimacing faintly as her muscles protested

She picked up the cup of tea Jane had poured for her and wrapped her hands round it, warming their coldness.

'You could say that I took your advice, regarding my problem with David Randal,' she told Jane lightly, and then added in a shaky voice. 'Or I could say that I behaved in a way so totally out of character that even now I can't believe what actually happened.'

'Oh, what "actually did happen"?' Jane enquired, watching her. 'Or is that a question a sister isn't allowed to ask?'

'I went home with a man I met at the dance,' Sarah told her slowly. 'We made love. . .' Her eyes met her sister's. 'I wanted to. . .not just because of what we were saying the other day. I wanted him Jane—almost desperately.'

'Well, I'm very glad to hear it,' Jane said firmly. 'Who is he? Where does he live?'

Sarah put down her cup and looked down at the bedspread before replying. 'I only know his first name,' she told Jane in a low voice, stopping her before she could speak. 'That was all I wanted to know. I left last night while he was still asleep. The way he made me feel frightened me, Jane. I don't want to get involved. . .'

'You don't want to get involved, and yet you went to bed with him? Just how much more "involved" is there?' Jane demanded drily.

'I'm talking about involved as in emotionally involved,' Sarah told her. She moved restlessly in the bed, and then said tiredly, 'I don't want to talk about it, Jane. . .if you don't mind.'

Her sister got up and shrugged good naturedly. 'Well, you're over twenty-one and free to make your own decisions. . .but I hope you realise that your, er. . .partner in this little adventure, might not be as happy with a one-night stand and then a complete disappearing act as you are yourself.'

That thought had struck Sarah, but she was convinced that once he realised she had gone and did not intend to come back Joss would put her out of his mind. After all, he was an exceptionally attractive man, and one whose sexual experience could be in no doubt. There would be no shortage of women ready and willing to take her place in his bed. Who knew, it was more than likely that in the cold light of day he would be relieved to discover that she had gone. She daren't question too deeply why she should find that thought so depressing. The same fear she had experienced on first seeing Joss came back now to haunt her. . .it was impossible for anyone to fall irrevocably in love on so short an acquaintance she told herself firmly, and then shivered. In love? What on earth was she thinking of? What had happened last night had been the result of sheer physical chemistry, nothing more. It was over. . .finished. . . This afternoon she would be going back to London and her life there.

Ralph, tactful as always, made no comment about her disappearance, simply chatting over lunch about how pleased he was to have secured the new contract. When Sarah eventually left half way through the afternoon she felt as though she had restored some much-needed normality to her life. Indeed as she drove away from her sister's home, it seemed almost possible to convince herself that last night had never happened.

And that was the way it should be, she told herself firmly as her train carried her towards London. She had been privileged to share with another human being what for her had been a unique experience, and one, moreover, that would help to banish from her life David's unwanted attentions. Probably the main reason she had been so responsive to Joss was quite simply that at the back of her mind had been the knowledge that she was better off without her virginity. But somehow it was impossible to convince herself of this sensible explanation. Deep down Sarah knew quite well that the practical aspects of ridding herself of her virginity had been the last thing to motivate her, but it was too dangerous to admit the truth, too potentially painful to allow herself to remember the sensations Joss had helped her to experience, the pleasure he had given her. Determinedly she blanked out every single thought of him that tried to get past her defences. The best thing to do was to forget that last night had ever happened.

It was with that praiseworthy intention in mind that Sarah stepped into her office on Monday morning. The weekend was behind her now and so was everything which had happened during it. The arrival of a manuscript from one of her favourite authors helped her in this resolve. Sylvia Thornton was an enchanting seventy-odd-year-old who wrote delicate witty novels whose closest comparison must be those of Jane Austen and Sarah settled down with enthusiasm to read through her new manuscript.

She had barely got through the first chapter when her 'phone rang. Frowning slightly because she had asked her secretary not to put any calls through, Sarah picked up the receiver.

Steven Holland was on the other end of the line. 'Sarah, are you free for lunch?'

When she replied in the affirmative Steven said, 'Excellent. Come to my office when you're ready, will you?'

Feeling rather surprised, Sarah put down the receiver, glanced at her watch and discovered that it was close enough to one o'clock for her to lose no time in obeying Steven's request.

A quick check in the mirror in the ladies' reassured her that her appearance looked firmly businesslike. The suit she was wearing was neatly tailored, the soft peach colour a pleasant foil for her colouring. A tortoiseshell comb helped to keep her chignon in place, and after an application of lip gloss she felt ready to face her boss.

There was no one in the outer office when Sarah stepped into it, Steven's door was slightly open and she could hear him speaking to someone through it. She tapped on the door and waited. Steven opened it himself, beaming warmly at her as he ushered her into his office.

'Sarah, my dear, I'd like you to meet Joshua Howard. As you know he's taking James Richards' place. . . Joshua, I'd like you to meet our Women's Fiction Editor here at Leichner & Holland, Sarah French.'

As though she were an observer, standing outside her own body and watching the whole tableau, Sarah watched the tall dark man sitting

in the chair opposite Steven's desk, get easily to
his feet. The blood drained from her face in an
instant of blinding recognition which she knew
he shared, but more horrifying by far than the
realisation that Joshua Howard, her new boss, and
'Joss', her lover, were one and the same person
was the knowledge that it was not shock or fear
which had been her immediate emotional reaction
to the sight of him, but sheer and very intense
pleasure. In fact it had taken an immense amount
of willpower not to give in to the mad impulse
to run up to him, to... Terrified by her own
reaction Sarah looked blindly towards the
window, willing herself to wake up from what
could only be the very worst kind of nightmare,
but no, it was real enough. She could hear Steven
burbling away happily in the background, words
such as 'I'm sure the two of you will hit it off.
Sarah is an excellent worker...' impinging dis-
tantly on her consciousness, while overwhelming
and overpowering everything else was her
immediate and intense awareness of Joshua
Howard as a man. Even without looking at him,
even without going anywhere near him, she knew
him, she thought fatalistically. Her body seemed
to have some deep and hidden means of recognising him, and of registering that recognition to her.
All the fears she had subdued on the fatal night
of the ball now returned to crowd and oppress
her and the reality of them was far worse than
her imaginings. She closed her eyes momentarily

to block out the sight of him, and instantly realised it was a mistake. Instantly she saw him not as he now was, but as he had been. . .as her lover. . .

'Sarah and I have already met.'

The cool, confident claim made her eyes fly open and then desperately seek his. He was regarding her with a hard awareness that made her skin burn as she remembered how stealthily she had crept away from him in the darkness of the pre-dawn. His expression told her that he had not forgotten it and that he fully intended to demand an explanation of it.

'Oh?' Steven looked only faintly curious.

'Over the weekend,' Joss continued evenly, despite the fact that Steven had not asked for an explanation of his claim. 'I was in the country, checking on the work being done on the house I've bought there. Sarah and I met at a local event.'

'Yes. . .of course, I'd forgotten that your sister lives in the Cotswolds doesn't she, Sarah?' Steven asked her. 'How is the work coming along on your house, Joss?'

'Better than I'd hoped. With a bit of luck I should be able to move in pretty soon. The swimming pool is going to take longer to install than I'd hoped for.'

Listening to them Sarah felt her heart clench as she realised which house it must be that Joss had bought. Coming on top of everything else it was almost unbearable that he should have chosen for his home the one place she had long coveted and known to be out of reach, as her own.

'Come back, Sarah. . .' Steven teased her. 'You were miles away.'

She could feel the hot tide of colour crawling up over her skin and knew without looking at him that Joss was watching her. Did he think she had known who he was?

A brief, acutely painful glance at him told her that was not the reason for the anger she could almost feel emanating from him. She bit her lip as Steven ushered them both from his office. It seemed impossible that all that bitter fury she could feel emanating from Joss and directed towards her could be simply because she had quietly removed herself from his life. For both of them it had been an encounter without any commitment; and in all honesty Sarah could not see why he should have wanted one. So why the deeply burning rage she could sense burning inside him? Another and completely contradictory thought struck her, chilling her so much that she came to an abrupt halt in the corridor, shivering slightly. What if it was not because she had so abruptly exited from his life that Joss was so bitterly furious but because of the totally unexpected way in which she had re-entered it?

The idea made too much sense to be dismissed, and although she was conscious of a degree of curiosity in Steven's eyes as he touched her arm lightly and directed her towards the lift, she could not let the idea go. Obviously, when he had held her in his arms and whispered his desire for her, when he had made love to her physically and verbally, Joss had not had the slightest idea that they would be working together. Neither of them had, but Joss was, in effect, now her boss. Was he thinking that she might use what had happened between them, or was he simply angry because he felt he had revealed something of himself to her that he would not normally have revealed to a lower ranking colleague?

If so. . .how did he think she felt? Hot colour burned her skin as Steven guided her into the lift. She could feel the heat coming off Joss's body as she stood in close proximity to him, her eyes resolutely looking at the lift doors. He was willing her to look at him, and with such an intensity that she could almost feel the skin at the back of her neck burning, but she refused to give in to it. By the time the lift stopped a fine film of sweat had broken out on her skin, panic flaring wildly to life inside her.

Somehow, she managed to endure the ordeal of lunch, although afterwards she was never sure what she had eaten or what had been said.

At one point on the way back to the office Steven commented cheerfully, 'I'm sure you two will get on. Sarah's a very sensitive and gifted editor, Joss, I think you'll find her invaluable.' He glanced obliquely at Sarah and added knowingly,

'And I'm sure you'll find Joss a great help too, Sarah, especially when it comes to dealing with writers like David Randal.'

Sarah was powerless to prevent the slow surge of heat suffusing her skin at the mention of David's name. She wondered if she was the only one to be aware of the peculiar tension that seemed to hang in the air. Unable to stop herself she glanced at Joss and saw that he was watching her, a grimly unreadable expression in his eyes.

It was only when they stepped back into the building that she felt able to breathe properly again. No doubt Steven would now whisk Joss off to his office and she would be left alone to come to terms with what had happened, giving her a breathing space she badly needed.

The only sensible thing for her to do now would be to hand in her notice, but how could she? She was committed, at least for the next few months, until money came in from Ralph's new contract, to helping out with the expense of keeping Gran in her comfortable new surroundings. With the memory of how happily the old lady had settled in there still fresh in her mind Sarah knew that it would be impossible for her to give up her well-paid job. She would just have to remind herself that Joss was as unlikely to want to discuss what had happened between them as she was herself. . .but for far different reasons, she admitted wryly as they all stepped out of the lift. She was not so stupid that she wasn't aware of the reason for that totally unexpected flare of joy the sight of him had brought. It hadn't just been a mere sexual attraction she had felt towards him; she was forced to admit that now. . .and also to acknowledge that the reason she had been so reticent with him had been to protect herself from the danger that any further exposure to him was almost sure to bring. Now it was too late for that; she had been brought face to face with the truth of how strongly she was attracted to him; of how deep the emotional commitment, she had unwittingly made to him, went.

It had been all very well to disguise the truth under the banner of the necessity of losing her virginity when she had been safe in the knowledge that she was never likely to set eyes upon him again, but now that provided scant protection.

She was profoundly grateful when she reached her office door, relief turning to shock as she heard Joss saying evenly to Steven, 'If you don't mind I'd like to spend some time with Sarah this afternoon, discussing one or two things. . .'

Steven beamed his approval, obviously taking Joss's comment as an indication of his goodwill towards her, Sarah thought numbly, wondering how Steven could be so blind to the rage she could see so clearly smouldering in the dark blue eyes.

There was nothing she could do. She had to smile mechanically and open her office door to him as Steven left them to it.

There was no sign of Katy, her secretary, and then Sarah remembered that the other girl had a dental appointment. Biting down hard on her lower lip she opened the door to her own office. Small at the best of times, it now seemed positively claustrophobic. She turned round and discovered that Joss was immediately behind her, leaning indolently against the closed door. But there was nothing at all indolent about the way he was looking at her, and she shivered in the grip of primitive fear.

'Now. . .' he said softly, not making even the slightest concession towards his claim to Steven that he intended to discuss work with her. 'Just what in hell are you playing at?'

Anger had darkened his iris almost to purple-black. There was a rigidity about his body that made her own tremble, and yet she forced herself to stand up and face him rather than sink down into her chair as her shrinking body ached to do.

She licked her dry lips nervously, her body tensing in instant shock as he crossed the space that divided them and shook her fiercely.

'Don't do that, damn you,' he told her thickly. 'What the hell are you trying to do to me. . .send me out of my mind? Why did you leave like that? Why. . .?'

She must keep calm, Sarah warned herself. Whatever else happened she must not let him guess the truth. She thought she knew why he was so angry now. It was a combination of the shock of discovering her here. . .and the blow to his pride her disappearance must have caused.

It had not occurred to her before that he might feel that her disappearance was a rejection of him.

'Why did you leave like that?' he demanded again. 'Do you know what I went through when I woke up? I had no idea you were a virgin until it was too late to. . .to stop. Did I hurt and frighten you so much that you felt you had to run away from me, Sarah?' His voice was having a mesmeric effect on her. He had already stopped shaking her but he had not moved away and now his fingers touched her jaw, tracing her bones. Something inside her flared painfully to life and she wanted nothing more than to be in his arms— but for how long?—an inner voice asked her. For how long would he want her? He was an experienced man. . .she was not the first woman he had desired. . .and she was already far too vulnerable to him to give herself in a relationship whose end she could already forecast. She didn't want Joss for a brief interlude, she acknowledged painfully, she wanted him for ever.

'I thought I'd made it good for you, Sarah.'

There was so much pain in his voice that she could not stop herself from saying huskily, 'You did.'

'Then why. . .? Why leave like that. . .? If it wasn't for the coincidence of our meeting today like this, I'd never have seen you again, would I? Would I, Sarah?'

He was shaking her again, his words falling on her like blows. She had to defend herself from him somehow, Sarah thought desperately. If he continued like this she would admit the truth to him. The bitterness and anguish he seemed to be experiencing hurt her so much. There was nothing she wanted more than to tell him how she felt, but the vulnerability she sensed in him now was not real; he was a powerfully sexual man only made weak by a momentary desire that would fade far, far faster than her own acute love.

Slowly, an escape route opened up before her. Taking a deep breath Sarah spoke slowly, unable at first to look directly at him as she said quietly, 'No, Joss. You wouldn't.'

'Am I allowed to ask why?'

Sarah shrugged forcing herself to meet his eyes now and appear calm. 'Does there have to be a reason? I thought it was understood by both of us that what happened was a—'

'A one off,' he bit out cruelly. 'It was certainly a unique event in my experience. . .and, of course, in yours,' he reminded her savagely. 'If you don't mind my saying so, I find it rather strange that a woman in her mid-twenties, who's still a virgin, should suddenly take it into her head to go to bed with a complete stranger.'

'Haven't you ever heard of instant attraction?' Sarah said flippantly and wished she had not when she saw his eyes narrow and harden.

'Instant attraction, like love at first sight, is the

corner-stone on which a firmer relationship can be built, but you didn't want anything other than exactly what we had between us, did you, Sarah? You simply wanted—'

She couldn't bear to listen to any more. If he said another word she would disgrace herself completely by bursting into tears in front of him. How on earth could she have been so foolish in the first place?

Summoning all her courage she said grittily, 'I simply wanted you to remove the burden of my virginity, Joss.' She had to turn away from him so that he would not see the lie for what it was; and apart from that, the quality of his tension unnerved her. It was as though he had been carved from stone. Even his breathing seemed to have stopped.

'You see I've been having problems with one of my writers. He seems to have developed a fixation about my virginity.'

'So why go to bed with me and not him?' Joss demanded crudely.

She couldn't let him see how much this was costing her. . .how much pain she was being forced to inflict upon herself.

'Because for one thing I do not find him in the least attractive—far from it—for another he's married. . .and for yet another I dislike his brash assumption that I should warm his bed, simply because he desires it.'

Speaking slowly as though he wanted every

word to be clearly understood Joss asked her,
'Are you telling me that you went to bed with me
simply to stop another man from desiring you?'

No. . .no. . .never. . .her heart cried, but Sarah
silenced its cry.

'Perhaps that's rather over simplifying matters,
but yes, in essence, that's correct.'

The silence that followed seemed to stretch for
ever and then at last Joss said curtly, 'So what
now? When do you plan to flaunt your night of
debauchery in his face?'

The acid way he bit out the words burned into
her with soul-shrivelling pain. He was making no
attempt to conceal his contempt and anger. She
badly wanted to cry, to plead with him to understand that she couldn't tell him the truth; that she
was terrified of admitting even to herself just how
much he already meant to her. It was pride and
pride alone that kept her standing there, her voice
as cool as she could make it as she replied.

'I'm hoping that I shan't need to. Don't they
say a man can always tell when a woman he
wants has another lover?' She spoke as derisively
to him as he had done to her.

'Do they?' He laughed with a soft savagery
that froze her muscles. 'Well, it certainly helps
if there are a few clues to go by as well.'

The way he hauled her into his arms made her
tense in instant fear—a fear which she had never
come near to experiencing on Saturday night. She
wanted to weep for what they were doing between

them to the memories she cherished, but it was too late for tears. . .too late for explanations. She gasped in a mingling of shock and pain as she felt Joss's teeth bite into the soft skin of her throat, the rough movement of his mouth against her skin arousing her despite all her attempts to pretend it was not.

He released her as roughly as he had seized hold of her. She saw that he was breathing hard, as though he had been running, a dull flush of colour running up under his tan.

'Now,' he told her thickly, gripping her chin with unkind fingers. 'Now he will know at least that you have been touched by passion.' His eyes hardened as he added with a venom that made her body ache with pain, 'I hope for your sake he doesn't react the same way to this,' his fingers touched her throat, burning her skin, 'as I wanted to do when I woke up on Sunday morning and found you gone.'

He paused in the doorway to her office, his eyes glittering febrilely as they refused to let her look away.

'It was all nothing more than a cheating fake from start to finish wasn't it, Sarah? All of it.'

She desperately wanted to tell him the truth, but pride compelled her to say huskily instead, 'What did you expect?' Her mouth twisted. 'That I'd fallen madly in love with you?'

His smile was cruel as he responded softly. 'I wish to God you had because believe me I can think of no sweeter means of revenge right at this moment in time.'

Revenge! The cold bitterness of the world held her rigid by her desk long after he had gone. She must have damaged his pride more than she had ever imagined. . .surely not because she had left him? No. . .because of the lie she had told him, Sarah told herself emptily. How on earth was she going to be able to work for him? It just was not possible.

She looked at her desk, her glance falling on the manuscript she had begun that morning with such enthusiasm. Now all she wanted to do was to crawl into a dark safe place and hide—preferably for the rest of her life.

CHAPTER FIVE

THE realisation that Joss was to start work with them the following Monday only served to depress Sarah further. She must be the only person in the entire company who had not gone down with Joshua Howard fever, she reflected bitterly, after a particularly trying lunchtime during which she had had to endure her colleagues' paeans of praise and intense speculation about their new Editor in Chief.

'Having been a writer himself he'll know exactly what to look for,' Rachel enthused to Sarah over their afternoon coffee.

'Not necessarily.' Sarah knew she sounded brusque and that Rachel was staring curiously at her, but she couldn't help herself. She was still agonisingly raw inside from the verbal mauling Joss had given her on Monday. With each hour that passed she dreaded the coming week. . .how on earth could she work alongside him? It was impossible. . .and yet how could she leave?

Rachel had just left her office when Katy popped her head round the door and grimaced faintly. 'I thought I'd just warn you that David Randal's on the premises. I saw him come out of the lift just as I left the ladies'.'

David! That was all she needed right now. Instinctively her hand went to her throat and the betraying mark Joss had left there. Today it was discreetly covered with a silk scarf. Colour stung her skin as she remembered her shock on discovering just what he had done to her. Fortunately now the bite was fading.

She forced herself to concentrate on the work on her desk, hoping that David would leave her alone.

After Monday's shock meeting with Joss she was surprised that there was anything left that could overset her, Sarah found herself thinking wryly, but the sensations Joss's lovemaking had aroused inside her had given her a new insight into David's aggressiveness. Now that she had known for herself the full power of sexual desire she did not find it as easy to dismiss David's threats as she had done before.

She knew the moment he walked into her office, prickling darts of awareness running along her skin. She had his manuscript on the desk in front of her, together with a list of the amendments she wanted to discuss with him.

He strolled in carelessly, exuding an air of sexual aggression that she could almost reach out and touch.

'Well. . .and how's my beautiful Sarah? You've thought about what I said to you the last time I was here, I hope.'

Sarah cringed beneath the gloating tone of his

voice. David was already anticipating his own victory. A shudder of distaste convulsed her body at the thought of him so much as touching her—the sickness she had known before, only intensified now that she had known Joss's lovemaking.

She looked up in time to see David's eyes narrow and harden as he witnessed her automatic revulsion. A hard flush of colour stained his skin, and with the afternoon sunlight pouring into her room he suddenly looked exactly what he was. A middle-aged man, well past the best part of his life, his face pouchy, marked indelibly by the life he had led. There was nothing kind or reassuring about him, Sarah thought tensely. Everything about him repulsed and yes, frightened her. She recognised within him an ego that would never forgive her for rejecting him; and in addition to the lure of her virginity part of his desire to possess her was founded on that rejection. He wanted to subdue and punish her, Sarah recognised, and the knowledge made her suddenly and acutely aware of how vulnerable she was.

Telling herself that she was being ridiculous and that not even David would attempt to force himself on her in her own office, she gave him a calm smile and picked up the manuscript.

'I've read through it again, David, and there are several points I want to discuss with you.'

She could see the flush of rage on his face, because she had ignored his threat; and fear pierced through her, sharp and entirely female.

Gripping the notes she had made Sarah fought for self-control. If she let David see he had frightened her. . . Her mind shied frantically away from the danger that suddenly seemed to yawn in front of her. Today she could sense about him a barely leashed rage and instinctively she knew he was only waiting for an excuse to give that rage physical expression. He would hurt her if he touched her now and enjoy hurting her. Just as he enjoyed the degradation he enforced upon his heroines, Sarah realised, recognising now exactly what it was about the supposed 'love' scenes in his books that she always found so distasteful.

The knowledge which had come to her so swiftly made it easier for her to confront him, her voice calm and reasonable, as she asked him to sit down.

'I was going to write to you about your manuscript, David, but now that you're here. . .'

'I haven't come here to talk about the damn manuscript and well you know it. I want you, Sarah. . .and I want you badly enough to go ahead and take you if you keep on playing games with me like this.'

Now, thankfully, anger came to her aid, banishing her fear. Standing up, her face flushed with temper, Sarah faced him.

'*You* are the one who's playing games, David. I've told you right from the first that I have no sexual interest in you whatsoever. *You* are the one who keeps on raising the matter. I never have, and never will have any desire to become your lover. . .'

She saw the dark colour mottle his skin but banked down her apprehension. 'And we both know why that is, don't we?' he sneered. 'You're frightened of being touched by a real man. . .or at least you like to pretend you are. There are a hell of a lot of women like you, Sarah, who say no—when they really mean yes.'

Anger touched her nerve endings in electric currents. She could scarcely contain her rage at David's arrogance and bull-headedness.

'When I say "no", I mean it,' she told him fiercely, 'and so do the rest of my sex. That's something you might do well to remember when you're submitting your heroines to what in actual fact is enforced rape. It might help boost your dropping sales if nothing else,' she told him blightingly.

Immediately Sarah realised she had put herself in fresh danger. David had never liked having his work criticised and in the past she had always been too unsure of her own ground, of her own judgment, to force the issue. Now she was beyond that. A woman herself, she knew what her sex wanted to read in their novels, and it was not some sick man's fantasy of what. . .of what he would like to do to her, Sarah recognised on a wave of nausea as she recalled one particularly unpleasant passage from his latest manuscript, which had involved the captive heroine being tied up and forced to endure an act which Sarah now recognised from her own experience had been entirely one-sided and completely without pleasure for its female victim. No wonder David's books were no longer selling so well. If she thought about it she could see that gradually over the last couple of years, the sexual passages in them had become more and more sadistic.

'You bitch.' He almost spat the word out at her, practically bellowing with rage. 'And just what the hell do you know about it. . .a frigid little virgin who was only put in the job because—'

The door to her office suddenly swung open with controlled force. Because she was facing the door Sarah saw Joss first, her eyes widening with shock and—yes—relief as he strode into the room. She hadn't realised he was visiting them today, and immediately hated herself for the weak feeling of relief seeing him brought.

'What the hell's going on in here?'

He spoke without inflexion, his voice controlled and quiet and yet Sarah was immediately aware of the power behind it. David got to his feet, in what Sarah recognised as an instinctive attempt to dominate the younger man.

'And just who the hell are you?' he demanded to know.

'Joss Howard.' Joss introduced himself coolly. 'The new Editor in Chief.'

A wary light crept into David's eyes, he looked from Sarah's pale face to Joss's implacable one and then shrugged and smiled charmingly at Joss. 'I was just saying to Sarah—'

'I heard exactly what you were saying to her,' came back Joss's clipped response. His eyes flickered momentarily, resting briefly in Sarah's pale face. 'And for your information,' his voice dropped an octave, smooth and thick as melting honey, stirring up memories Sarah could very easily have done without, 'I can tell you she is neither frigid, nor. . .' he paused and looked at Sarah, smiling at her in a way that made her toes curl into her shoes and heat shoot through her veins, 'any longer a virgin. . .'

Before Sarah could react Joss moved, coming to stand behind her, one hand resting on her shoulder, in the lightest of touches, and yet one so proprietorial that she could see the immediate reaction in David's eyes.

Anger glittered sharply there as his eyes moved from Sarah's face to Joss's. Sarah had the unnerving feeling that if Joss had not been there to protect her David would have physically assaulted her. She had always known of his desire to possess her, but never guessed at the frightening intensity of it before now.

David got up. 'I've another appointment in fifteen minutes,' he said curtly. 'I'll have to go.'

It was Joss who escorted him out of her office, leaving Sarah feeling as though she had just survived some terrible cataclysm.

She was still sitting staring into space ten

minutes later when Joss came back, still trying to accept that he had actually done what he had. . . that he had, despite their quarrel earlier in the week, protected her from David.

'Here, drink this.' He pushed a carton of coffee under her nose but until she touched it Sarah hadn't realised that she was shaking.

'Charming company you keep,' he said curtly, watching her. 'He, I take it, is the would-be lover you were telling me about?'

'Yes.' There seemed little point in denying it.

'Mmm. . . And this?' He gestured to the manuscript on her desk.

'His latest novel. . .'

Some of her distaste must have shown in her voice because Joss frowned and picked up the manuscript. 'From now on I'll deal with him,' he told her flatly.

Instantly colour surged up under her skin. There was nothing she wanted to do more than to thank him, but stubbornly she felt that she must master her fear of David. . .that dealing with his manuscripts was part of her job and that if she let herself be terrorised and brow-beaten by her authors she would not be worthy of the trust Steven had placed in her.

'No.' She said it sharply and watched his eyebrows draw together, repeating more softly. 'No. . .he's one of my authors, I must deal with him myself.'

She couldn't look at Joss. If she did he would

see how very much she wanted him to refuse to let her. The very thought of facing David again made her shrink in acute fear.

'How long have you been having problems with him?'

Joss walked over to her window and stood with his back to her. She had no way of seeing his face, but his voice was clipped, almost angry. Sarah sighed. She could not blame him for his anger. Here he was just about to start a new challenging career, and already he was being faced with personality clashes. It was her job as an editor to get along with the writers in her orbit; to smooth out problems and avoid strife.

'Right from the start,' she admitted huskily, knowing it was pointless to lie. 'When he first came in with his latest manuscript, six months ago.'

'And all this time you've said nothing to Steven?'

He was looking at her now, anger leaping across the distance that separated them, his eyes a deeply biting blue.

'How could I?' She spread her hands in a gesture of helplessness. 'Steven gave me this job against James Richards' advice. I wanted to justify his faith in me. If I had told him that I couldn't handle David. . .'

His mouth curled in acid disdain as he said softly, 'Hasn't it occurred to you yet that if you had complained to Steven right at the start this whole thing could have been nipped in the bud. As it is now. . .' He frowned, and slid his hands into the pockets of his immaculately cut suit.

'From now on, if you have to see him, it will only be in the company of another member of the firm—preferably male. I don't like the man,' Joss added, 'but I haven't been here long enough yet to judge how important his work is to the firm, and that must always be the prime consideration.'

He was looking at her as though he expected her to argue with him, but Sarah looked back proudly. 'I quite agree,' she told him coolly.

'So, how important is it?'

She was floundering now. 'James Richards thought very highly of him,' she said weakly at last. 'He has had quite a degree of success.' She gnawed at her bottom lip, wanting to give a balanced and well-judged opinion that did not involve her own emotions.

'But. . .' Joss prompted, lifting one eyebrow as she stared at him in confusion.

'Come on, Sarah, it's obvious that there *is* a "but",' he drawled. 'So what is it?'

'David's work is aimed primarily at the female market. Just lately sales seem to have been falling off.' She bit her lip nervously. 'I'm not happy with certain aspects of his latest work. . .I want to discuss them with him.'

'Discuss them with me,' Joss ordered, sitting down in the chair David had vacated and picking up both the manuscript and her notes, and reading quickly through the latter.

'Mmm. . . So you don't like the way the sexual passages of the book come across, is that it?'

Sarah nodded her head. A strange sensation of heat seemed to be consuming her body. She wished Joss was not quite so close to her. . .that she did not feel so weak.

She knew she had had every reason to feel tense when he drawled softly, 'Do you think you have sufficient experience to base these criticisms on?'

She knew quite well he was not talking about her professional experience and hot colour stained her skin, her eyes widening and darkening, and then gathering herself together she said brittly, 'Maybe not before. . .but now, yes. . .'

There was a long silence, and then at last Joss said, 'I see. . .' He stood up and picked up the manuscript. 'I think I'll read through this for myself.'

He paused by the door, and Sarah looked up at him in a daze. What could she say? Thank him for his timely interruption and for his totally unexpected lover-like attitude towards her. She touched her tongue to dry lips and stammered, 'Thank you for what you did. . .for. . .'

'For what?' He shrugged carelessly. 'I only told him the truth, and after all, that he should learn it was the whole purpose of your making love with me, wasn't it, Sarah? It would have been a pity to waste all that effort.'

He left her feeling as though she had been physically assaulted. Every muscle in her body ached—with tension she realised numbly, and yet he had rescued her. He could have simply walked past her office door. . . She shuddered violently as she dwelt on what might have happened if he had. David's maddened face swam before her eyes, and a sudden surge of nausea attacked her stomach. What on earth had made her refuse Joss's offer to take the author off her? Pride, she admitted wryly. . .pride and the knowledge that she could not afford to be seen to fall down on the job—she needed it too much. How did she know that Joss was not already plotting to get rid of her? He couldn't possibly want to work with her. . .his apparent act of kindness could have cloaked an ulterior motive. He might have used David against her to prove to Steven that she wasn't professionally capable.

On Thursday evening Sarah rang Jane, as she did every week. Her normally calm sister sounded both flustered and excited. 'You'll never guess what,' she told Sarah. 'The Merryweathers have invited us all to spend a week with them in their villa on Menorca—and that includes the brats. It's all going to be a bit of a rush though, we leave on Friday evening. Apparently there are still some details about the contract that Tom wants to sort out with Ralph, and because they're

spending the next month in Menorca suggested
that we join them there.'

'Jane, that sounds lovely.' Sarah was pleased
for her sister. It had been a long time since Jane
had had a proper holiday.

'Mmm, there'll even be a maid, apparently, to
keep an eye on the kids. Luckily we're all well
stocked up with summer things, and Tom is paying for our flights because it's "business".' She
gave a very un-Jane like giggle. 'I just don't know
whether I'm on my head or my heels. Anyway,
how are things with you?' Jane asked at last.

Sarah had already resolved to say nothing to
her about Joss. 'Fine,' she lied brightly. 'Rather
hectic. . .our new Editor in Chief starts next
week.'

She was glad that Jane had something else to
occupy her mind otherwise Sarah was sure her
sister would have guessed that something
was wrong.

They chatted for several more moments, and
then saying that she realised that Jane must have
loads to do, Sarah rang off.

Her small flat, normally so warm and homely,
seemed to stifle her tonight. She prowled her sitting room restlessly, consumed by a hectic energy
that needed an outlet. Even though it had happened two days ago she had still not got over the
shock of her interview with David and Joss's
totally unexpected interruption. She gnawed tensely on her bottom lip. She was grateful to Joss

of course. . .but beneath that gratitude tension still lingered. The more she thought about it the more she felt sure he would contrive some way of getting rid of her. After all, he could hardly want her working with him, could he?

Friday was a busy day and Sarah was conscious of a rare sense of desolation as she listened to her workmates discussing their plans for the weekend. Normally she quite enjoyed the weekends she spent in London. In winter she toured the art galleries; in summer the parks, and in the past she had always relished her solitude, enjoying her role as an observer; she got plenty of participation in life when she went down to Jane's, but now it struck her for the first time that all her experiences of life were coming to her secondhand. . .all bar one. . . She shivered slightly in her centrally heated office, glad that there was no one there to see the betraying surge of colour running up under her skin when she thought of Joss.

Now it seemed impossible that they had ever been lovers; on the two last occasions she had seen him in the office he had seemed too chilly and remote. . .apart from those few brief seconds when he had played the possessive lover for David's benefit.

Her 'phone rang and she picked it up automatically, brightening when she heard Steven's voice.

'Come down to my office for a minute would you, Sarah?'

Wondering why he had summoned her, and remembering the last occasion on which he had done so, she took the time to renew her lipstick and comb her hair before doing his bidding.

This time, however, he was in his office alone. Disturbed by the intensity of her disappointment Sarah told herself she had been ridiculous in imagining that Joss might have been there in the first place. They all knew that he wasn't due to start working with them until Monday, despite his appearances in the office this last week.

Steven was facing his window when she walked in. He turned round and she saw to her dismay that he was frowning slightly. An even-tempered, very fair man in general, Steven occasionally suffered from black moods. All of his staff had learned to tread warily when they saw the warning signs of these rare occurrences.

'Joss has just been on the 'phone to me,' he told Sarah without preamble, still frowning, although to her relief Sarah sensed that it was something unconnected with her personally that was disturbing him.

'It seems he's not going to be able to join us here at the office until next Wednesday at the earliest. One of the contractors he's employing on his new house is behind on the contract and Joss wants to stay in the Cotswolds until the job's completed.'

Sarah could appreciate Steven's concern, but surely it hardly involved her to any great degree.

She soon discovered just how wrong she was.

'It seems that Joss had already scheduled a good deal of office work for his first few days here. He's already read his way through most of our current list, but he hasn't touched on any of your stuff yet, and he wanted to get that done before he decided what, if any, alterations he wanted to make in the departments under his control.

'Have you got anything planned for this weekend, Sarah?'

Puzzled she shook her head. 'Nothing at all.'

'Ah, that's good.' For a moment his frown lightened. 'Joss wants you to go down to this house of his and to take with you your current list, plus any manuscripts you've earmarked for possible publication. I did point out to him that that involved asking you to work over the weekend,' Steven told her before she could speak. 'You know how I feel about asking my staff to take on extra work without proper notice.'

Sarah did. Steven was a stickler for fairness, and believed in being scrupulously considerate to all his employees, which was probably why he had so few staff problems, Sarah reflected. Although she had often had to work late, or take work home with her, it had always been at her own instigation. Steven had a firm rule that said that people needed to play as well as work.

'I did suggest to him that you might go down on Monday, but it seems he's anxious to get on with checking through your list as quickly as possible. Apparently he had intended to call in here this afternoon and collect it from you. . .I must admit that a couple of days is not really long enough for him to get through it. . . How do you feel about giving up your weekend, Sarah?'

She shrugged. 'It needn't come to that. I could drive there and back in the day, tomorrow. I know the area very well. My sister—' She broke off as she realised how uncomfortable her boss was looking, frowning slightly herself as he studied her with pursed lips and thoughtful eyes.

'It seems that Joss needs more from you than mere carrier duties,' he told her at last. 'As a one-time journalist and writer himself he's familiar with the basic run of our list. . .but he feels that when it comes to the women's fiction side of things he doesn't have the experience to make any judgments. He feels that if you were there to go through the list with him, explaining to him the reason for what has previously been chosen—backed up by the sales figures—it would give him a much clearer idea of exactly what we look for on the women's fiction side. I can see the sense of that, of course.'

So could Sarah, but she could also see something else. Suppose Joss wanted to go through her lists to try and use it as ammunition against her. . .to try and prove that she wasn't fit to hold down her job? Panic flared inside her, which she quickly subdued. How often had Steven chided her before for her lack of confidence? Their women's fiction list might only be short, but the last quarter's sales figures from the work they had published had been most encouraging. . .and all those books had been Sarah's own personal choice. In fact, on a couple of them she had had to battle extremely fiercely with James Richards to get his acceptance of them. He had wanted to go for more of the 'bodice ripper' type novels that David produced, but Sarah had held out for her own choices. In one case this had meant publishing the work of a hitherto unknown author—James had been adamantly against this—but the sales figures so far had proved Sarah to be right, and Elaine Phillips had already been commissioned to write a follow-up to her first book for them—a historical saga, following the fortunes of a Yorkshire family down through the ages. James had complained that the book lacked 'fireworks', by which she suspected he meant sex. . .but it had a quiet charm that held the reader's imagination and in Sarah's view readers would be eager to follow up the first book in the series by reading the second.

'Sarah. . .' She realised that Steven was still awaiting her response. Every instinct she owned urged her to be wary of Joss. . .not to be intimidated by him.

'If Joss wants me there while he goes through the list then I'm quite happy to fall in with his wishes,' she told him coolly.

Immediately his frown lifted. 'Good girl,' he approved. 'What will you do...stay with your sister?'

Sarah bit her lip. That was something she hadn't thought about. 'I'm afraid that won't be possible,' she told Steven. 'Jane and her family are going away on holiday.'

'Don't worry about it...if Joss wants you down there, he can sort out some accommodation for you,' Steven told her with a smile. 'I'll give him a ring now, and then let you know what the arrangements are.'

Sarah made her way back to her own office her mind buzzing, fuelled by a determination to prove to Joss that although she might not be able to cope properly with David she was a thoroughly professional editor.

That was the problem in being the youngest and only female editor employed by the firm, she reflected wryly back in her own office. The other editors were sometimes inclined to patronise her, and she, ever-conscious of the weight of her new responsibilities often found it hard to speak up for herself. But she was a good judge of what other members of her sex wanted to read. She need have no fears on that score, the sales figures from her list proved that. And yet it was a heavy responsibility...and her own faith in her own judgment was not entirely secure. If it was, she would have told David immediately that she did not like his new novel. It worried her that Joss seemed to have picked out her list for such intense scrutiny. The story he had told Steven seemed reasonable enough but Sarah was not reassured. She would have to be on her guard if this was the opening round of a campaign to undermine her position with the firm. Joss would make a daunting adversary. . .

Her 'phone rang and she picked up the receiver.

'Sarah? Everything's fixed up,' Steven told her. 'You're to stay with Joss. Apparently he's got plenty of room. . .and as he says it will make it much easier for the two of you to get through the work on hand if you're there on the premises, so to speak. You have got a current driver's licence haven't you?'

Numbly Sarah confirmed that she had. Stay with Joss? Now why should that thought intimidate her so much? Because in staying with him she would be giving him the advantage of being on his own home ground, she thought grimly, and Joss Howard had far too many advantages on his side already!

'Good. Luckily we've got one of the rep's cars in the garage at the moment. You can use that. . .' He caught the note of surprise in her voice and chuckled. 'Well, it's the least we can do since you're giving up your weekend. It wouldn't have been much fun for you struggling across London with two dozen or so books in your suitcase, not to mention half a dozen or so manuscripts.'

That was something Sarah had not thought

about. Thanking Steven for his consideration, and listening to him telling her that he would have the car filled with petrol, and that she could pick up the keys from Bill, the maintenance man, as she left for the evening, she tried to quell the sense of dread filling her.

It would be stretching coincidence far too far to imagine that Joss had deliberately arranged matters this weekend so that they would fall out as they had. . .but it did seem that fate was giving him a very unfair lead on her.

Well, she would just have to show him that she was not as easily intimidated as he no doubt believed. It was very unfortunate that he should have walked in on her and David when he did. . . and she would have felt that way about the scene he had overheard even without the additional complications of the fact that they had been lovers. All in all it was probably hardly surprising that he was so anxious to get her out of the firm, Sarah thought wryly. Even without the personal conflict between them on a professional showing to date she had scarcely done anything to inspire his confidence in her.

It was just gone six when she left her office. Bill grinned at her when she went down to the door, clutching a box of books.

'Mr Holland told me to expect you, Miss,' he assured her. 'Car's outside and waiting for you. . . tank's full. Mr Holland said to tell you that Mr

Howard would be expecting you this evening,'
he added, as he took the box from her and turned
to open the plate glass door.

This evening! Sarah digested that in silence
as she hurried back to her office for the rest of
the books.

Another two journeys had the new list's manuscripts, plus all the sales charts, safely installed
in the boot of the car, which she carefully locked.

The car was a nippy Metro, bright red and only
one year old, although with a fairly high mileage.
Bill saw her comfortably installed inside it, and
after one or two bumps as she got the feel of the
clutch, Sarah drove smoothly out on to the main
road. She had deliberately delayed leaving, knowing that on a Friday night the traffic would be at
its heaviest between four and six. Now it was still
heavy but not too bad to cope with.

Luckily, she was a quietly confident driver,
refusing to be flustered or provoked, using caution where she thought it necessary as she refused
to yield to the impatient honking of a sports car
driver who apparently wanted her to pull over. . .
no doubt so that he could go through the lights
at red, Sarah thought in mild irritation, wondering
as she did so what it was about being behind the
wheel of a car that seemed to change some
people's personalities.

It took her just under half an hour to get to her
flat. Luckily it was in a self-contained block with
its own tiny gardens and car park, so she had no

problems as to where to leave the car.

Once inside her flat she took her time about getting ready. She had no idea what time Joss expected her, but she wasn't going to allow his high-handed actions into panicking her.

She showered and washed her hair, and then while she was waiting for it to dry she made herself a salad meal. In all honesty she knew that she wasn't hungry, and that in a way she was simply employing delaying tactics. She didn't want to have to face Joss and she certainly did not want to be alone with him. . . Thank God he was not still living in the cottage. Her face flamed as without wanting to she had a vivid mental picture of them both; their naked bodies entwined, hers both inciting and yielding to the powerful masculine dominance of his. . .

Shuddering slightly she fought to deny the image, pushing away her salad barely touched, and trying to turn her mind to more practical things. She would need to pack. . .what should she take with her. . .? Common sense suggested the kind of casual clothes she normally took home with her when she stayed with Jane but she was staying with Joss as a subordinate employee— she would be working. Chewing on her bottom lip she went to her wardrobe and quickly extracted a couple of pastel-hued skirts and their matching blouses—outfits she normally wore for the office but which were a little less formal than her business suits.

She put these in the case and then added jeans and T-shirts and then clean underwear and a nightdress. She would hardly need anything else.

When her hair was dry she dressed slowly in clean underwear, a fluid printed cotton skirt and a matching plain top comfortable enough to drive in, but not so casual that Joss would not recognise her businesslike approach to the coming weekend. Since she nearly always wore her hair loose at weekends, instead of twisting it up into her office chignon, she compromised by making one long neat plait which she secured with a tortoiseshell clasp. It was much cooler with the heavy weight of her hair free of her face and neck like this, she thought, studying her reflection in the mirror as she applied a light glossing of eyeshadow and lipstick.

By eight-thirty she could delay no longer, and besides she was sensible enough to realise that if she did not leave soon, it was going to be past midnight before she arrived at her destination. She grimaced faintly at the thought of having to knock her host up out of bed. Joss would not be pleased. No doubt he had expected her to go rushing down there straight from the office, she reflected wryly, terrified out of her little mind by the thought of displeasing him. She suspected that her inability to handle David successfully had given Joss a contempt of her professional abilities in general. If she wanted to keep her job—and she did—she would just have to reverse that

impression. . .and she was going to start by showing Joss that she was not at all afraid of him!

It was only as she got into the car that she
realised that she was at last going to realise her
teenage dream of occupying Haughton House,
even if it was only briefly. Smiling rather grimly,
she started the car. So many other things had
happened to her since the last time she had
seen the house, that her passionate love for it
as a teenager had completely faded into
obsolescence. . .

CHAPTER SIX

Joss was not in bed when she arrived, and neither was he alone. A scarlet Mercedes sports car was parked next to his Porsche, and as Sarah brought the Metro to a halt, she wondered why Joss had been so insistent that she drive down tonight, if he was already entertaining guests.

She got out of the car and went up to the front door to ring the bell. From outside it was impossible to see what work had already been done to the house. Problems with the contractors had been Steven's explanation for Joss's inability to return to London.

The front door opened, and Sarah stepped through it to confront her host. He was dressed in black pants and a white shirt; the shirt opened at the throat, his hair faintly disordered. For some reason her mouth went dry, and she had to fight to drag her gaze away from him.

'You took your time.'

So. . .there was to be no chivalrous respite. Battle was already engaged.

'I'm not a fast driver,' she responded with equanimity, 'and I didn't leave town until nearly nine.'

'You don't need to explain. . .I hardly expected

you to come rushing down quivering with eager anticipation.'

His choice of words disturbed her, as she was convinced they meant to conjure up, as they did, memories of an occasion when she had literally quivered with eager anticipation and she was grateful for the lack of light in the hall to hide her expression.

She was just growing accustomed to its dimness when a light, feminine voice called out impatiently, 'Joss, what on earth are you doing, darling?'

Now even more than before she was glad of the shielding darkness. No need any more to wonder about the racy Mercedes parked outside. Was this another deliberate move on Joss's part— reinforcement of how little desire he had to promote any further intimacy between them? Punishment for the surely very small dent she had made in his pride? Loweringly, the thought struck her that Joss was hardly likely to be affected by her feelings one way or the other. Why should he want to show her that there were other women in his life? That there must be had already been perfectly apparent to her.

The owner of the voice came tapping impatiently on high heels into the hall. In its dim light Sarah saw the pale glint of her expensively coiffured blonde hair. She came towards them, ignoring Sarah to link one slim tanned arm through Joss's.

'Darling,' she purred huskily, 'you're keeping me waiting. . .' Red lips pouted seductively and with a small shock Sarah realised that despite the skilful make-up the woman was much older than she had first thought—closer to her mid-thirties than her mid-twenties. Only the faint lines on her skin betrayed that fact, though. Her figure was as slim as a girl's, her pink cotton jumpsuit, with its zip open to her breasts, something that Sarah herself would have thought twice about wearing.

An extrovert; used to getting her own way. . . and very, very determined under that little girl pose, Sarah suspected, waiting politely in the shadows for Joss to introduce her.

'Ah. . .but keeping you waiting makes you all the more eager, Helene,' he drawled softly, flicking the beautifully modelled nose with one finger.

The blonde pouted again, and made a husky sound of pleasure deep in her throat. Sarah suspected that the other woman was trying to embarrass her, but it wasn't embarrassment she was feeling, it was. . .it was nothing she told herself sternly. . .and certainly never, never jealousy. What right did she have to feel that sort of emotion? None. . .none at all. . .

'Who's your little friend, darling?' the blonde asked at last, when Joss made no attempt to introduce them.

'A member of my new staff,' Joss told her laconically.

'Oh.' The tone of the blonde's voice changed.

'I see. . .one of the secretaries I suppose. . .' Her voice trailed away, dismissively. Sarah felt her skin prickle with dislike.

'Actually, no.' She could tell by the amusement in Joss's voice that he was enjoying her discomfort and moreover that he was perfectly aware of her resentment. 'Sarah is the editor of Leichner & Holland's women's list.'

'Oh.' If anything Helene's voice was even cooler.

'Sarah come and be introduced to an old friend of mine, Helene Standish. You might know Helene rather better under her stage name—she's Rosemary Parish.'

Sarah recognised the latter name immediately. She had seen the actress in several television plays and had not liked the open sexuality she always seemed to bring to her roles.

Even so she hid her aversion and extended her hand formally murmuring, 'Yes, of course. . . I've seen you on television.

'And with a bit of luck you'll soon be reading her first novel,' Joss told her smoothly, ignoring his companion's slight pout.

'Darling. . .I thought we agreed that we wouldn't say anything about my book until it was finished.'

'Well, since it will be included on Sarah's list. . .'

His casual assumption that a manuscript that she herself had not even seen yet was already on her list infuriated Sarah, but she hid her anger and said instead, 'It sounds extremely interesting, Miss Standish. I'll look forward to reading it.'

'It's Mrs. . .actually,' Helene told her icily. 'I've retained my married name even though I'm now divorced. . .but I'm sure there won't be any need for you to read my work, er. . . Sarah. Joss will do that. To be honest I prefer a man's opinion. . .'

Sarah was sure she did, but even so she could not resist saying sweetly, 'For women's fiction?' Her eyebrows lifted slightly. 'I admit there are some excellent male editors of the genre but they're very few and far between.'

Helene was looking at her as though she was having trouble believing her ears, her silvery laughter faintly forced as she exclaimed, 'Good heavens Joss, you're going to have to teach your staff who's boss, I think. By the way. . .what is she doing here?'

So she was reduced to 'she' now was she, Sarah thought grimly, awaiting Joss's explanation with a certain amount of acid pleasure.

She was not disappointed.

'Sarah has brought down her list for me to oversee,' Joss told Helene briefly.

Icy blue eyes flashed dangerously over Sarah. 'I see, so that's what you meant when you said you were going to be busy this weekend, darling. . . This new job must be awfully important to you.'

The insult behind the words was staggeringly plain, but Sarah refused to respond to it.

'I am,' Joss agreed.

'Well, remember, darling, that I expect you to come down and stay with me later this month. I should have finished the first draft by then and I want you to go over it with me. It's such a nuisance that I have to fly back to Cannes tonight... and such a pity that you can't come back with me.'

She was looking at her, as though she personally were responsible for that fact, Sarah reflected, wondering what Helene would say if she realised how dearly Sarah would love to see Joss go with her. Probably never believe her, Sarah thought wryly. What woman worthy of the name would pass up on an opportunity to have Joss all to herself?

No sooner had the thought formed than Sarah dismissed it. She had no right to any personal interest in Joss whatsoever, she reminded herself. None at all. And yet it was impossible not to feel jealous as Joss slid his arm round the other woman's shoulders and guided her back through the hall, calling over his shoulder to Sarah to follow them.

She *couldn't* love him...it was impossible that she should...and yet she did... It hadn't been simply desire or propinquity that had urged her to go with him the night of the ball...somewhere deep inside herself she had instinctively recognised him as the man she would love. . . She could come up with no rational explanation for this, but nevertheless it was true. She had gone with him because not to do so would have been impossible. . .and yet it would have been far, far better if she had not.

She followed Joss into a large shadowy drawing room and was suddenly and very bitterly angry with him, instinctively she sensed that he was deliberately highlighting for her benefit the sexual relationship that existed between himself and Helene. Almost instantly the hot heat of her anger changed into sick misery. Could this really be the same man who had held her in his arms; who had made love to her in a way that. . .but no, she wasn't going to think about that. She mustn't think about it.

Instead, she studied her surroundings, seeing that the large drawing room was filled with various oddments of furniture, none of it apparently of any particular age or style. She came out of her reverie to hear Helene saying to Joss,

'Darling, this place is such a mess. I don't understand why you're insisting on staying here. Surely it would be much better to stay away until the work is finished. . .'

'If I could trust the contractors to keep to their time schedule then, yes, it would be, but unfortunately I can't, which is why I, and incidentally Sarah, are here.' He stood up and glanced at his watch.

'Didn't you say you had to leave for your flight?'

'Unfortunately, yes. . .' Again the pout. 'Come and see me off then, darling and then you can get on with your work in peace.'

Again she linked her arm through Joss's, making no attempt to speak to her, Sarah noticed, but she wasn't really bothered. She heard their footsteps ringing across the tiled hall, the front door opened and then there was silence. A silence that stretched for a considerable length of time. Unwanted and tormenting mental images slid treacherously into her mind. It was all too easy to picture Helene in Joss's arms. . .

Eventually she heard a car engine fire, and then within a few seconds Joss was back. Sarah blinked as he switched on the main light. In its glare she could see how shabby the elegant room was. She knew that Joss was coming towards her, but she kept her attention fixed firmly on the fireplace, refusing to look round.

'You've brought everything I asked for with you?'

Sarah knew that she should have been relieved by his businesslike manner, but contrarily she was not. Politeness if nothing else demanded that she at least look at him as she gave him her confirmation, but she wished she had not when she saw the lingering imprint of Helene's lipstick against his jaw and mouth. So what had she thought they were doing ouside. . .discussing their mutual work?

'Everything's in the car,' she added tiredly. 'If you'll tell me where you want it, I'll go and bring the boxes in.'

'It can wait until the morning.' He glanced at his watch again and frowned. 'It's gone midnight. . .I expected you earlier.'

'Well, it's lucky that you were disappointed then, isn't it?' Sarah responded with a cool mockery that surprised herself.

'Meaning?'

She hadn't expected his dulcet challenge and had to fight to stop the betraying colour flooding her skin, as she forced herself to meet it.

'Meaning that had I arrived earlier you would have had less time with Helene.'

He smiled tigerishly and said softly, 'Jealous, Sarah?'

She had a momentary and insane desire to strike out and destroy the smiling mockery on his face, but fortunately managed to control it. How dare he change tracks like this, twisting her remarks so that their conversation had turned from the impersonal to the personal, she wondered despairingly, quite forgetting that she had been the first to make the challenge. Banking down her anger she said coldly. 'Of course not. . . how could I be?'

For a moment she thought she saw something akin to anger cloud his eyes, but it was gone before she could be sure—his voice as cool but much drier than her own as he agreed. 'How, indeed?'

'To experience jealousy one must first love,' Sarah protested doggedly, determined to have the final word.

'Where did you learn that little home truth?' He was almost snarling at her now. 'From someone else's writing. . .certainly not from personal experience, eh, my little virgin. . .'

The taunt hurt, sliding through her guard like a rapier through tender skin, reaching to where she was most vulnerable. As she battled against betraying her pain she saw the sardonic expression in Joss's eyes. He had won this encounter, she would have to give him that, she acceded painfully to herself.

'I'm rather tired, Joss,' she said not troubling to hide the weariness that suddenly seemed to have dropped over her. 'If you could tell me where I'm going to sleep.'

He smiled again, not kindly, and opened the door behind him.

She followed him automatically, stopping half way up the stairs as though the breath was driven out of her lungs when he threw laconically over his shoulder, 'What if I told you you were sleeping in my bed, Sarah?'

She could feel time tick relentlessly by as she fought against the insidious memory of his hands on her body, his mouth against her skin. Slow shudders of remembered pleasure built up inside her, threatening to destroy her self-control.

'That would be fine,' she managed to say at last. 'Just as long as you were sleeping somewhere else.'

He waited until they were both at the top of the stairs before making any comment, turning slightly towards her so that his face was in the shadows and hers was not. It was almost eerie, listening to his voice without being able to see his expression properly.

'You're a liar, Sarah,' he told her quietly, 'and I could take you to my bed right now and prove it to you.'

It was only the suddenly prickly sense of danger that gave her strength to say coolly:

'And you, Joss, are a very arrogant man. I'm not going to deny that I found pleasure in your lovemaking—I did. . .but I've already told you why I went to bed with you and that statement still stands.'

She held her breath waiting for his response, but all he did was move ahead of her down the shadowy corridor, stopping outside one of the several doors.

'Sorry about the poor lighting,' he apologised laconically as he pushed open the door.

'The electrical contractors are half way through rewiring. The kitchen and most of the downstairs are done, but they haven't got this far yet. . .

'None of the bedrooms have been touched I'm

afraid—I got someone up from the village to clean this one for you. . .'

Sarah stepped past him and grimaced faintly at the brightly hued, old-fashioned wallpaper, but as he had said, the room was clean, the bed looked comfortable, if somewhat old-fashioned, and after all she would only be staying a few nights.

'No private bathrooms as yet, I'm afraid,' he continued, going back to her bedroom door, 'the only one in use is there.' He pointed to a door across the corridor. 'And in case you're wondering it has a lock on the door. Is your case still in the car?'

'Yes.'

'I'll go and bring it up for you. Luckily my study has been finished. So I suggest we get to work down there early tomorrow morning. . .say ten-ish?'

Sarah nodded her head, studying her new surroundings as he went back downstairs for her case.

The room was a pleasant size and had the potential to look extremely attractive. She was dreamily mentally re-furbishing it when Joss came back.

He dropped her case on her bed and then walked over to the door, pausing briefly to drawl, 'Sweet dreams, Sarah,' and then he walked through it and closed it after him.

Since she had heard him walk back downstairs, Sarah judged that it was quite safe for her to use the bathroom. She had no wish to be caught at the disadvantage of dashing across the landing by Joss when she was only wearing her nightdress.

The bathroom was as old-fashioned as her bed-room, but thankfully there was plenty of hot water. She showered as quickly as she could, removing her make-up and brushing her teeth, before gathering up her discarded clothes. It was a nuisance that she had no dressing gown. She didn't need one at the flat, and it hadn't struck her that she would not have the privacy of her own bathroom. Mentally shrugging, she unlocked the door. Her nightdress was made of soft cotton, and was surely modest enough for her not to need to feel so concerned that Joss might glimpse her in it...after all, he had already seen what lay beneath it. And not just seen, she reminded her-self, caught off guard by the slow burn of heat flooding over her body.

Despite her physical tiredness it took her a long time to get to sleep. Her searingly painful jealousy on seeing Helene with Joss was something she was going to have to come to terms with and accept. Frowning slightly, Sarah acknowledged to herself that it really would be much safer from her point of view if she could find another job... but she had already sworn to herself that she would not allow Joss to browbeat her into leaving Leichner & Holland, and besides, she could not afford to. But every second she spent in his com-pany only added to the trauma and pain she would

have to face, when eventually he was no longer
there. How could she bear to work with him,
when she knew there were other women in his
life, when she ached to touch him the way she
had done tonight. She would have to find a way,
Sarah told herself resolutely. . .and who knew,
perhaps in doing so she might also find a way to
destroy her love for him as well. He was not the
embodiment of all her secret inward yearnings as
he had seemed that first night. . .he was a man
who could be cruel, as he had been tonight. She
should be feeling glad that she had had this
glimpse of the man he really was, but instead, all
she could feel was pain.

She woke up early, so early that a fine spring
mist still clothed the fields in the distance. Seven
o'clock. . .far too early to start work and she had
never felt less like sleep. On impulse she got out
of bed and made for the bathroom. Ten minutes
later she was pulling on jeans and a T-shirt, and
on her way downstairs, her hair secured in its
plait, her face free of make-up.

After a certain amount of trial and error she
found the kitchen, taking in Joss's study on the
way. His study was really a small library, with
some beautiful mahogany shelves running along
one wall. The whole room had a decidedly
pleasant masculine ambience from the richly
coloured Persian rug on the floor to the heavy
partners' desk with its leather chairs.

It would be very pleasant to work in an atmosphere such as this. . .especially on a cold winter's afternoon, Sarah thought, noting the large marble fireplace. If she closed her eyes, she could almost smell the scent of apple logs. . .

Sighing faintly, she went in search of the kitchen, gazing appreciatively around its spaciousness. Plainly no expense had been spared in its remodelling, and Sarah guessed that it had once been several smaller rooms. She liked the solid oaken units and the tiled worktops, and the ceramic tiles on the floor.

She was longing for a cup of coffee and she opened a few cupboard doors experimentally, discovering a washing machine hidden away behind one set and a fridge-freezer behind another. Eventually she managed to locate a filter coffee maker, and some coffee, although from what she could see, Joss had not yet got round to stocking up his cupboards.

He obviously hadn't expected to move into the house as yet, she reflected, remembering what Steven had told her. While she waited for the coffee she looked for some bread to make toast with, but could find none.

By the time she had poured and drunk her coffee it was gone eight o'clock, and she was still hungry, Sarah thought wryly. She opened the fridge door and investigated its contents, frowning over their paucity. How did Joss envisage they were going to live over the next few days?

She remembered that the local village shop opened early on Saturdays, and on impulse decided she might as well use her time advantageously, rather than simply waiting for Joss to come downstairs.

The woman behind the counter recognised her and looked slightly surprised to see her. 'I thought your sister was away,' she commented, when Sarah gave her her order.

'She is.' It was plain that the woman was curious, but Sarah did not explain, simply smiling her thanks as she packed away her groceries.

The shop did not sell bread, but by the time Sarah had left the village store, the small, family run bakery had opened.

The delicious smell wafting through the open door was far too tempting to resist. Sarah went in and emerged several minutes later carefully carrying a bag containing freshly made croissants, and another with still-warm wholemeal bread.

She had no idea what, if any, plans Joss had made for their meals, but at least she would not starve, she decided cheerfully as she started up the Metro.

A little to her surprise there was still no sign of Joss when she returned.

It was gone nine o'clock now and she still had not had her breakfast, and according to Joss they were starting work at ten. Shrugging mentally and telling herself that it was no part of her duties to act as Joss's unpaid housekeeper, Sarah set about making fresh coffee, and then her conscience smote her. It wouldn't kill her to go upstairs and ask him if he wanted a drink. She had turned the oven on to warm her croissants, and the smell filling the kitchen was making her practically dizzy with hunger.

Sighing faintly, she hurried upstairs, stopping abruptly when she realised she did not even know which was Joss's room. As she hesitated she heard the bathroom door open and she turned round, her eyes widening slightly as she took in the powerful breadth of Joss's shoulders; the tiny droplets of water that still clung to the smooth suppleness of his skin. Helplessly her glance skittered over his body, naked apart from the towel wrapped round his hips. A great wave of intense longing hit her, obliterating everything else, including the reason she had come upstairs in the first place.

'That's no way to look at a defenceless man, Sarah.'

The mocking words filtered past the shock of seeing him and remembering. . . The hand she had automatically lifted to touch his skin fell to her side, her face white with shock. It was impossible for her to speak; her throat seemed to have closed up completely, the weakness washing over her, frightening in its intensity.

'Breakfast. . .' she managed to say weakly eventually. 'I. . .I didn't know if you were awake. . .if you wanted any breakfast. . .'

'Breakfast. . .' He laughed softly. 'And what were you proposing to give me, sweet Sarah? The bewitching nectar of your mouth? The honey sweetness of your skin?'

At his words a deep, flooding tide of aching desire spread through her body. He was making love to her as surely and as effectively as if he were touching her, Sarah thought despairingly, and she was powerless to stop her body's response to him.

'You want me, Sarah. . .' The arrogant certainty in his voice brought her back to sanity and reality, desire changing to bitter anger as she looked at him and saw the mockery in his eyes. Suddenly she wanted to hurt him as badly as he was hurting her. Her anger was so intense that it blotted out everything else, she moved instinctively, reacting to the pain tearing at her, only realising what she had done in the thick silence that followed the sound of her palm against his skin. In sick dismay she looked at the spreading imprint of her hand, her eyes cloudy and dazed, unable to accept that she had actually hit him. Suddenly, the dangerous elemental quality of the silence enshrouding them struck her and she took a step backwards, but Joss moved faster, imprisoning her wrists with cruelly hard fingers, no trace of amusement or mockery in his eyes now. They were as dark and unreadable as the deepest ocean and she shivered beneath their cold bleakness.

'Don't take your frustration out on me, Sarah,' he told her grimly, shocking her with the brutality of his judgment. 'At least not in that way. . . What's the matter?' he goaded softly, watching her with eyes as merciless as those of a falcon guarding its prey. 'Too shy to ask for what you really want?'

This couldn't be happening, Sarah thought despairingly. Why, oh why, had she come upstairs? Why hadn't she stayed in the kitchen where at least she had been safe? She gave a small moan, a release of pain both physical and mental, closing her eyes as she tried to blot out the sight of Joss's bitterly derisive face.

'Don't do that, you little fake.' He muttered the words against her ear, causing shivers of fear to spread through her. 'We both know this haunted pallor and mock martyr air are false. No woman hits a man unless she either wants him to hit her back or kiss her. . . Now which was it, Sarah? Are you going to allow me to make my own choice?'

She struggled then, tugging desperately to be free, hating him for what he was doing to her and hating herself as well, for her inability to forget what it had been like to be held in his arms as a lover.

It was pointless to struggle. He dragged her against his body, freeing her momentarily to secure her there with the arm he closed round her waist, holding her so tightly against him that it was too dangerous to struggle. His free hand imprisoned the back of her neck, his mouth descending to hers with punishing fierceness.

His grip on her was so tight that she could feel his heartbeat thudding into her body; the heat coming off his naked torso; the male strength of him compared with her own vulnerability. And she could also feel the potent force of his desire. It made her go weak with tormenting memories, her mouth opening beneath his, reality fading.

Humiliatingly it was Joss who dragged his mouth from hers, lifting his head and breathing hard as he muttered savagely, 'Oh, my God. . . that. . .'

His harsh voice was all it took to remind her of the truth. His grip had slackened sufficiently for her to pull away from him, which she did, her body trembling as she forced herself to say huskily:

'I came here to work with you, Joss. . . Nothing else.' Tears blurred her vision as she continued shakily, 'You can believe that or not as you choose, but I want it clearly understood that I do not want you to—'

'Make love to you?' His mouth twisted, as though he was having difficulty in believing what she was saying and fully intended her to know it. And why shouldn't he? She couldn't hide from herself never mind him the fact that she had responded to him just now with unmistakable hunger, and she hated herself for it.

'I don't even want you to touch me. . .' she
told him fiercely, stepping back from him.

He was looking at her with a peculiar intensity,
his skin surely paler than it had been? Frowning,
Sarah glanced down at herself, tensing as she saw
the way her T-shirt clung to her body, clearly
revealing the tormented thrust of her breasts and
nipples, the fabric damp from its contact with
Joss's body.

She took a couple of steps backwards, and then
for no reason that she could analyse later when
she was calmer, flung at him bitterly, 'You can
believe what you like but I did come up here to
see if you wanted any breakfast.' And then, before
her composure deserted her completely, she fled
back downstairs to the kitchen.

The warm, yeasty scent of the croissants, which
had so tormented her taste buds earlier, now only
made her feel sick. She switched off the oven
and sat down at the kitchen table, her head in her
hands. She couldn't stay here if Joss was going
to torment her like that again. In his arms it had
been all too easy to forget all that had happened
between them since the night of the ball. In all
honesty she could not deny to herself that for a
few insane seconds she had actually wanted him
to pick her up and carry her to his bed. . .to make
love to her as he had done before. She shuddered
and forced herself to get up, and go blindly
through the motions of making herself fresh
coffee. . . How could she stay here now and work

with Joss? How could she not? She had her job
to think of.

He came into the kitchen several minutes later,
dressed as casually as she was herself, jeans
moulding the masculine length of his legs, a thick
cotton check shirt with short sleeves, snugly out-
lining his torso.

As he walked in through the door, he stopped,
frowned slightly and asked, 'What's that I
can smell?'

'Croissants and coffee,' Sarah told him list-
lessly. She couldn't bear to look at him. 'I was
hungry when I got up. . .I couldn't find any bread
and then I remembered that the village store opens
early on Saturdays. You didn't seem to have
much in the way of food. . .so I bought a few
things.'

He was silent and she couldn't bear to turn
round to face him. Now what she had done suddenly seemed unbearably encroaching. She had
no idea what plans or arrangements he might have
had in mind for their meals, she reminded herself.
With hindsight it was easy to see that she would
have been much wiser to stay hungry.

'Sarah. . .'

She felt the light touch of his fingers on her
shoulder and tensed.

'I'm sorry. . .I owe you an apology for what I
said earlier.'

For what he'd *said*. . . but not for what he'd
done, Sarah noticed, forcing herself to turn to

face him. She managed a careless little shrug as she slid away from his grip.

'That's all right,' she said coolly. 'I don't suppose it's any more your fault that you're used to women inviting themselves into your bed, than it's mine that I'm not. . .'

'Mmm. . .rather ungrammatical but I get your point. This time I'll let you get away with your acid little barb, Sarah. . .but don't try pushing me too far.'

Her stomach was quivering like jelly but she refused to let him see it.

'What else did you buy besides croissants?' he asked her, carelessly opening the oven and removing them. 'I had intended to go out and get some supplies later on, but it seems that you've saved me a chore.'

'Only the barest necessities,' Sarah told him. 'I wasn't sure what sort of eating arrangements you had in mind.'

He sat down and put the plate on the table. Now he looked at her, frowning slightly. 'Meaning what exactly?'

Sarah shrugged. 'Well, if my sister had not been away I would have stayed with her and only come here to work. I don't know what social commitments you may or may not have.'

'Meaning that you really believe I'd leave you to eat here alone while I was swanning off wining and dining elsewhere?'

'I'm here as an employee...not as a guest,' she reminded him stiffly.

'And as your boss it's my duty to see that you're properly fed,' he retorted blandly, adding with a faint grimace, 'There's so much work for us to get through. I was rather hoping you wouldn't mind if we took it turn and turn about to organise our meals. It will be chaotic I know... with the contractors here and everything else. I had no intention of moving in at this stage, and so I haven't even attempted to engage any staff. However, if you prefer it I can arrange for you to eat at the local pub if my company is such anathema to you.'

What on earth could she say? If she insisted on eating alone now she would be childish and petulant.

'I've only got enough food to last us the week-end,' she told him eventually.

'Then first thing Monday morning we'll go and get some more. These croissants are delicious,' he added, biting into his second. 'Aren't you going to have one?'

'I'm not hungry.'

But in the end she did eat one, and she cooked Joss bacon and eggs. A dishwasher meant that there was no need for them to wash up but Sarah couldn't help herself from smiling slightly when he said,

'Well, I suppose I'll have to make lunch... what did you plan for us to have?'

'Chicken salad,' she told him gravely, watching the laughter leaping into his eyes.

'I think I might just about manage that. . .or I could, if you're very good, make you my *pièce de résistance*, this evening instead. Steak *au poivre*. . . I'm very good at it, and I happen to know there's some fillet in the freezer.'

'Okay you're on. . .'

It was deliciously heady stuff, sharing this teasing banter with him but it was also very dangerous, Sarah reminded herself as she followed him into the study. The boxes from her car were standing beside his desk, and as she sat down at it she could almost feel him distancing himself from her.

Nervous now, knowing that he would soon be judging her professional ability, Sarah rummaged through the boxes for the financial statements of last year's list.

They worked until lunchtime, Joss painstakingly thorough as he listened to her explanations of her reasons for last year's choices, sometimes making notes, sometimes not.

When she had finished he asked her, 'And how do you feel about the books you chose last year, in view of the financial statements on their sales?'

He was asking her to substantiate with figures, her choices, Sarah realised. She took a deep breath.

'There are one or two surprises,' she admitted hesitantly. 'The saga, which I personally liked, but wasn't too sure would have mass appeal, sold extremely well. . .so well that we've commissioned a follow-up. James was disappointed that David's book didn't do as well as he'd hoped. I know that Steven is very well pleased with the profit on the women's fiction list so far.'

Joss waited a few seconds and then said evenly, 'I asked you for *your* opinion Sarah. *Your* opinion of your own judgment. . .or don't you feel able to give me such an opinion?'

He was coming dangerously close to uncovering her vulnerability concerning her self-confidence and Sarah could not allow that.

'So far I'm quietly pleased with my success rate,' she told him calmly.

'Quietly pleased?' One eyebrow rose. 'That's something of a contradiction, isn't it? Why aren't you loudly pleased, Sarah? It's my experience that most editors are only too eager to let others know just how well they've done. . .just how invaluable they are to their employers.'

What was he hinting at? That she wasn't to think herself invaluable? Was he deliberately trying to undermine her; because he was certainly succeeding.

'I said quietly pleased, Joss, because that's exactly what I meant,' she told him firmly. 'I haven't been doing the job for long enough yet to be any more confident than that. Of course I'm pleased that my choices have done so well, but that isn't enough to tell whether it was good judgment on my part, or simply good luck.'

'I couldn't have put it better myself,' Joss agreed drily, plainly amused to see her fall into the pit she had dug for herself. 'And the only way we will have of knowing will be to let you select this year's list and possibly next's. And, of course, if it was only good luck and that luck fails. . .'

Sarah wanted to protest that he was hardly being fair. But she was too unsure of her ground to do so. She felt instinctively that she did have a flair for her work, but she was naturally unassuming and hesitant to take credit for herself without someone else there to back her up in doing so.

'Steven seems to have confidence in me,' she said stiffly.

Joss grimaced. 'Steven is a sucker for a pretty face,' he told her blightingly. 'Which is one of the reasons he's more than happy to hide behind me and let me be his hatchet man—if, of course, it should ever come to that. . .as I was just saying, it's really early days as far as your abilities are concerned, isn't it? Now I think we'd better break for lunch.'

Childishly, Sarah wanted to tell him that she didn't want to eat. He had thoroughly upset her, leaving her feeling tense and drained.

Joss was watching her and Sarah felt thoroughly unnerved when he said softly, 'Hasn't it ever occurred to you that you're somewhat on the sensitive side for this job, Sarah? How do you cope for instance when you have to deal with a stubborn writer, when you have to ask for alterations or do I already know the answer to that?'

Sarah knew that he was referring to David Randal.

'That's not fair,' she burst out, very close to the verge of tears. 'Most writers aren't a bit like David.'

'I should hope not,' he agreed blightingly, adding: 'By the way, I've been through his manuscript, and I don't like it. It takes an attitude to women that could do us a great deal of harm as a publishing house from a feminist point of view. He'll either have to abandon, or re-work.'

'I'll tell him.' Her relief that Joss agreed with her own view of David's book was swamped by the knowledge that she would have to confront David again.

'No.' Joss's sharp refusal jarred through her. '*I'll* tell him,' he told her grimly. 'Somehow I think it will be much more effective coming from me. . .'

His eyes told her mercilessly exactly what he meant and Sarah quailed beneath the derision in them. He was undermining her authority again, and she knew she had to object, and yet a cowardly part of her wanted to hand over the responsibility for dealing with David to him. . .

'It's my job—' she began only to fall silent as Joss intervened crisply.

'And it's mine to see that yours gets done, as quickly and efficiently as possible. You'll have to forgive me, Sarah, if I say that I can hardly see that being accomplished after what I witnessed in your office the other day. David Randal terrifies you.'

It was all too uncomfortably true, and Sarah lapsed into an unhappy silence. In a few short hours Joss seemed to have possessed himself of every one of her weaknesses. . . How long would it be before he told her that he intended to recommend to Steven that she was demoted? Not very long, she suspected miserably.

'Come on, lunch.'

The fresh salad and chicken might just as well have been sawdust, Sarah reflected as she pushed her plate away, barely touched. If this was a sample of what working with Joss was like, then perhaps she ought to give in her notice. But how could she? How could she let him see that he had bested her? How could she manage without her salary?

They were two questions that returned again and again to torment her in the days that followed.

Joss had a capacity for work that she could only marvel at, and she could not hide from herself the knowledge that he was an extremely able and accomplished editor. Somehow in the few days he had available he managed to read all through her past and current lists, possibly in bed at night, Sarah reflected, because he was certainly far too busy to do so during the day. If they weren't being interrupted by the contractors, the telephone was ringing. . .it amazed Sarah how quickly he could switch his attention from one thing to another without apparently losing track. The more she saw of his own professional ability, the more insecure she felt about her own. He had given her the odd word of praise it was true. . .but all in all when she returned to London on Wednesday afternoon it was with the distinct feeling that her days as Leichner & Holland's women's fiction editor were numbered.

The very last thing Joss had said to her before she drove off was that immediately he got back he intended to write to David. 'If he gets in touch with you before then you can refer him to me.'

'And the work I'm doing on this year's list?' she asked hesitantly.

His response had been distinctly non-committal, and all in all Sarah was relieved to have been granted a couple of days off work, in lieu of the previous weekend, before she need face him again.

CHAPTER SEVEN

THE blow wasn't long in falling. She had been in her office for only half an hour on Monday morning when Steven rang through and asked to see her.

She could tell by the faintly embarrassed smile he gave her when she walked into his office what was coming. How easy it had been for Joss, she thought bleakly. She might have known she would not have had a chance in hell of standing out against him. What would Steven say if she told him that Joss wanted her out of the firm because they had been lovers? She closed her eyes, knowing she would make no such charge. . . and knowing just as much that it was true.

'Sarah, are you all right?'

She could hear the anxiety in Steven's voice. 'Fine. . .' she lied brightly. 'You wanted to see me?'

'Er, yes. . .' He fiddled with some papers on his desk. 'Joss and I were having a talk last week.'

'When I was away from the office. . .' Sarah said evenly.

She caught the vaguely shifty glance Steven sent her.

'Er. . .yes. That's right. Sarah, why didn't you

tell me about the problems you were having with David?'

She might have known Joss would choose to launch that cannon first, Sarah thought bleakly.

'I felt I should handle the situation on my own,' she responded coolly, wondering exactly how much Joss had told Steven.

'But to allow yourself to be subjected to such a degree of sexual harassment. My dear girl, you should have gone to James or myself immediately.'

'I couldn't,' Sarah told him baldly, 'David was one of James' pet writers.'

'Oh, yes. . .yes, of course, I'd forgotten that. . .' He picked a typewritten sheet up off his desk.

'When Joss came to join us it was on the understanding that he would be able to vet his staff and make whatever alterations he thought fit.'

Here it comes, Sarah thought numbingly, steeling herself for the blow. Why on earth hadn't she handed in her notice and left while she still had pride intact? She had known all along what would happen.

Steven was studying the sheet of paper in his hands. 'Joss is very impressed with the work you've done on our women's fiction list, Sarah. . . very impressed indeed.'

Silently Sarah digested the sugar knowing the pill was on its way. . .sensing the as yet unspoken 'but' she was sure would follow.

'But. . .' Steven continued, avoiding looking at her, 'he *is* concerned that you lack a certain. . . toughness shall we call it. . .when it comes to dealing with the authors. David is a case in point here—a rather extreme one I know—but you are a sensitive little thing, Sarah, I must confess I had no idea that you were having all these problems with David. You know, you really should have told me. Anyway. . .to get back to the matter in hand. For the time being Joss wants to take the women's fiction list under his own control. He suggests that to facilitate this you work for him as his personal assistant. . .you would still be responsible for the initial selection of the list. . . Joss would simply take over from you when it comes to dealing with the authors, and making the final choice. . .'

It was not what Sarah had expected. She blinked in bewilderment. . . Why on earth should Joss want her as his assistant? Unless. . .another thought struck her. No doubt he expected her to refuse the job. . .to hand in her notice rather than work for him, which would then totally absolve him, in Steven's eyes, for being responsible for her losing her job. Very clever, she thought bitterly. But it wasn't going to work. At this moment in time she was so keyed up and angry that she would have worked for the devil himself rather than give in to Joss's blatant manoeuvrings.

'Well, if that's what Joss feels is best,' she

heard herself saying huskily. 'I can't pretend that I'm not disappointed.'

'Of course. . .of course. . .' Steven soothed her, plainly relieved that he was not going to be faced with a bout of tears or protests, 'but it really is for your own protection, Sarah and there'll be no question of a reduction in salary.'

'That's very generous of you.' She said it mechanically, getting up out of her chair. The room swayed distressingly around her, and she was conscious of an empty aching feeling in the pit of her stomach. She hesitated at the door, knowing that right at this moment in time it would be impossible for her to face any one else, least of all Joss himself.

'I. . .I have a headache. . .' she fibbed at last. 'I was wondering if I might go home.'

'Yes. . .yes. . .of course you can, Sarah.' Steven was looking at her with concern. 'Please don't get upset about this. I promise you it's not a reflection on your ability and it won't be the only change Joss makes in the department. Once you've gained a little more experience in dealing with the authors you'll be back in charge of your own department.'

And pigs might fly, Sarah thought achingly as she stepped out into the spring sunshine several minutes later. All she wanted to do right now was to hide herself away from everyone. She could just imagine the gossip there would be when the news broke. How could she face the rest of the staff? She couldn't. She stopped abruptly on the pavement causing the woman immediately behind her to glare at her as she had to sidestep to avoid cannoning into her. And wasn't that what Joss was bargaining on. . .that her pride would not let her stay on with the firm in an inferior position. Oh yes, he had been very clever. He knew that Steven was far too sentimental and soft hearted to dismiss her outright so he had managed things so that she would leave of her own free will. . .but she was not going to do so. No. No matter what it cost her. . .she would work for him as his assistant, and she would make him regret the day he had suggested to Steven that she be offered that particular post, she thought viciously, as she headed for the underground.

By the time she let herself into her flat her fictitious headache had become a reality. All she wanted to do was to lie down, but she forced herself to strip off her office suit and blouse first, dropping thankfully on to her bed wearing just her underwear and waiting for the painkillers she had taken to take effect.

She was woken from a confused dream about Joss by the ring of the doorbell. Still muzzy from the painkillers, she staggered into the bathroom to pull on her towelling robe, making her way across the living room to the small hall.

She opened the door automatically and then

gasped with shock as she saw David standing outside.

'David!'

Too late she saw the expression on his face, her muzziness drowned out by the sharp spearing panic bursting into life inside her as he pushed past her and into her flat.

'Thought you'd been very clever, didn't you?' he demanded thickly waving a bundle of papers under her nose, 'getting that fine lover of yours to send me this.'

Sarah could only stare at him, frozen with fear and shock. What was David doing here? What did he mean?

'I suppose it was all your idea, wasn't it?' he snarled viciously, advancing so close to her that Sarah was forced to move backwards into her living room. She was trembling with an ever-increasing sense of disbelief and terror. She had no idea what David was talking about. . .but she could guess, couldn't she? He must have received Joss's rejection of his manuscript.

Her suspicions were confirmed when he continued vengefully, 'Well, you needn't think I'm going to leave it there. No one gets to make a fool of me. . .and believe me it's been tried by experts.' His mouth twisted and suddenly he was the most dangerous man Sarah had ever seen. Why had she never noticed before how small and close set his eyes were? How fleshy and repulsive his mouth. She closed her eyes and knew she had made a bad mistake as she felt his fingers dig into her shoulders.

'Thought you were so clever finding yourself another lover, and then getting him to get rid of me. . .didn't you? But not as clever as you thought. Why shouldn't I enjoy a little piece of the action you've been giving him. . .compensation for ruining my career? You frigid little bitch. . . You're too cold to appreciate real sex, either verbal or physical and it was your prudish interference that got my work rejected, don't think I don't know that.'

'You're wrong.' Sarah tried to sound firm, but knew she had failed. She tried to fight free of him, but his hold on her only tightened. . .a thick tide of dark colour was seeping up under his skin and she realised sickly that her fear was exciting him. Those scenes he had written into his books had been his own sick fantasies she thought, suddenly seeing the truth. . .and he would enjoy putting them into practice.

Rape was an ugly word. She had heard about women being attacked in their own homes and had wondered how it had ever happened. . .how they would ever be able to feel safe anywhere again. . .and now, she who had always been so sensitive to other people's fears, was experiencing that wholly feminine terror for herself. She wanted to scream and fight but she sensed to do so would only inflame him further. Reason with him. . .try and keep calm, an inner voice urged her, but it was like telling herself to climb Mount Everest equipped with nothing more than her own feeble strength.

Even so she tried. . .forcing herself to explain that she had had no real part in Joss's decision; that she hadn't even realised he had written to David.

'You're lying.' He said it so viciously that Sarah knew he did not want to believe her. He wanted to have an excuse to punish her—to hurt her—and she supposed that not even a man like David could rape a woman in cold blood. . .he had to have something to goad him. . .to use as an excuse to defend himself. She was trembling, and she could see his pleasure in her weakness. It was no use fighting. She closed her eyes against weak tears. Perhaps it would simply be better to let him get it over with and yet the moment she felt the fetidness of his breath against her skin, every muscle in her body clenched in desperate protest. If he touched her more intimately she would be sick. . .she knew it. . .

'Little bitch. Pretending to me that you were so innocent and pure when all the time. . . Enjoyed it, did you? Well, I'm going to enjoy making you pay for trying to make a fool of me. I needed to have that manuscript accepted. I needed the money it would have brought in. . .but you. . .'

He was whipping himself up into a state of intense fury, Sarah realised. . .panic flaring through her. . .

'Well, let's just see if you're as good as he obviously thinks you are.'

He was tugging at the cord securing her robe, and taking advantage of her freedom from the biting pressure of his fingers, Sarah broke free of him, tearing back into the hall.

He caught her in the doorway, exhibiting a speed she never expected, the force of his body weight slamming her back against the wall.

Sarah cried out sharply with pain, the breath jolting out of her body as she simply crumpled up like a broken doll.

'Stop that.' He hit her sharply across the face. 'Stop that noise. We don't want anyone coming to see what's going on, do we. . .?'

Spittle flecked his mouth and Sarah stared in fascinated revulsion as he dragged her up against the wall. It was a nightmare, it had to be. . .things like this simply didn't happen. But it *was* happening, she realised frantically a few seconds later, as David's weight kept her pressed against the wall and his hands groped with the top of her robe, wrenching it off her shoulders as he reached for her breast.

She felt the sickness gag in her throat as she screamed out a tormented denial of what he was doing and then she felt the sheer fabric of her bra tear, his fingers squeezing painfully at her breast as he leaned his full weight against her, grinding his hips into her body.

She was going to be sick, Sarah thought
dizzily. . .she. . .

'Sarah. . .'

The front door which David had left unlocked,
opened and Joss stepped into the hallway.

He took in the whole of what was going on in
less time than it took Sarah to draw the breath to
cry out his name.

With merciful speed the nauseating weight of
David's body was removed from her own. She
closed her eyes, dreading discovering that she
had simply imagined Joss's arrival—that in her
despair she was merely hallucinating—and then
opened them again as she heard the unmistakable
crunching sound of bone against bone, just in
time to see David sag to the floor, clutching his
jaw, his eyes wild with fury.

'She was only getting what she deserved,' he
swore at Joss. 'The little bitch has been leading
me on for months.' Spittle foamed against his
mouth now and although it made her sick to look
at him Sarah could not drag her gaze away. . .

'She wanted it. She was enjoying it.' David
was like a man possessed by a fever, his colour
high, sweat pouring off his skin as he staggered
to his feet. 'She wanted me, I tell you. . .'

Sarah saw the sick distaste in Joss's eyes. 'I'd
like to kill you for what you've just said and
done,' he said quietly, 'but the law doesn't give
me that right. . .it does, however, give Sarah the
right to prosecute you for attempted rape.

Where's your 'phone?' he asked Sarah without removing his eyes from David.

'No.' The denial was out before she could stop it. Sarah had heard what happened to women who brought rape cases to court. Often they were more mercilessly pilloried than their attackers. She couldn't endure to go through anything like that.

'See, I told you she wanted it. . .'

'No!' She shuddered in unmistakable revulsion, and then said huskily, 'Please make him go away, Joss. . .I think I'm going to be sick if you don't. . .'

'Don't worry. I'm already on my way. Leichner & Holland aren't the only publishers in the world,' he spat at them both. 'You wait and see, my book will make sales that'll make fools of both of you. . .I'll see you pay for what you've done to me both of you. . . As for that cold little bitch. . .' he sneered at Sarah as he moved towards her front door. 'You're welcome to her.'

'You shouldn't have let him walk away like that,' Joss told her quietly as he closed the door after him.

She tried to move away and make for the security of her sitting room, but she found she was too weak to move.

'I couldn't have gone through the trauma of a court case,' she told him huskily, shivering at the very thought.

'No. . .but it might have prevented him from succeeding in doing to someone else what he tried

to do to you. You realise he would have bloody
well raped you if I hadn't arrived when I did.'

Realised it! Sarah closed her eyes sickly. Even
now she was powerless to stop her mind from
relaying to her imagination tormenting mental
images of his hands against her body. . .his body,
engorged with lust, pressed hard against her own.

She swayed and heard Joss curse. From somewhere she found the strength to mutter weakly.
'I don't think he'd do it to anyone else. . .it was
just me. . .I never realised. . .' She shuddered
again and clung to the security of Joss's arms as
they closed round her.

'Perhaps you're right.' His voice came from
close to her ear. 'Where's your bedroom?'

She forced her eyes to open. 'No. . .' Her
mouth felt swollen and sore. . .and she raised her
hand to touch it, remembering how David had hit
her. She wanted to tell Joss that she didn't want
to lie on her bed before she had cleansed herself
of the contamination of David's touch. . .if she
did she would never be able to sleep there again.

'The settee. . .' she said groggily. 'I. . .'

She saw his mouth tighten. 'Don't worry,
Sarah, I wasn't about to finish what he started.'

It shocked her that he should think that had
even occurred to her and she shook her head. 'Not
that. . .I want a bath,' she told him shudderingly.
'I. . .I want to be clean. . .'

She heard him curse, but it was too much of
an effort to open her eyes to look into his face.

She felt him lowering her on to the settee, and shivered as his arms were withdrawn from her. All she wanted to do was to go to sleep, to blot out everything that had happened, but he wasn't going to let her.

'Where do you keep your booze?'

'I don't want a drink. . .' Her lip throbbed with pain and she raised her fingers to touch it, her eyes opening wide, when she felt Joss's fingers there instead.

'*You* may not, but I certainly do,' he told her unsteadily, holding her eyes with his own. 'You may not realise it but that's the first time I've hit another human being in anger since I left my teens behind. Dear God, that he should. . .I should have killed him.'

He said it so emotionlessly that Sarah blinked, conscious of the way the flat words hung on the air.

'What did he do to your mouth?'

'He hit me.' She saw the look in his eyes and shook her head. 'He's sick, Joss. He was enjoying it. . .enjoying hurting me. It was as though he was acting out one of his private fantasies. . .I know now why I've always disliked his books so much. . .I suppose instinctively I must have known that was the sort of man who enjoys hurting women. . .degrading them.'

'He ought to be locked up,' Joss said flatly, 'and if I had my way he would be. What was he doing here in the first palce?'

'He'd got your letter of rejection. He thought you'd done it because of me. . .he'd been to the office I suppose and discovered I wasn't there. . . it wouldn't have been hard for him to get hold of my address.'

'Not hard at all,' Joss agreed. 'It took me about five seconds.'

His comment made her frown. She had been so overjoyed by his timely arrival that it had not occurred to her to question what he was doing at her front door.

'Steven told me you'd gone home with a headache. It occurred to me that I might have been responsible for it. I thought I'd come and have a talk with you.'

'Try and persuade me to give up my job you mean,' Sarah said bitterly. Now that the shock of David's attack was receding she was remembering her earlier fears that Joss was determined to force her into giving up her job.

'Why should I want to do that?' Joss asked levelly. 'You must already know from what Steven told you that I consider your flair for fiction to be very well worth developing.'

'And that, of course, is why you've demoted me,' Sarah was stung into replying.

'Not at all. I demoted you, as you put it, to avoid just the sort of situation I found you involved in just now. . .although, of course, I never realised just how dangerous Randal is. As Steven told you, at the moment you're too soft with some of your authors—'

'And all you want to do is to protect me from them, is that it?' Sarah asked sarcastically.

Suddenly, horrifyingly she wanted to cry. She turned her head into the cushion of the settee, not wanting Joss to guess how appallingly weak she felt.

'Where the hell do you keep your drinks?'

Tiredly she gestured to a cupboard, relieved when he moved away from her. He had been too close to her before, making her too aware of the vast difference between him and David. Joss's body smelled clean and male. . .his breath fresh. . .his touch made her ache and burn for his lovemaking where David's revolted her.

'Here, drink this.'

Raw brandy, Sarah noticed, shuddering as she gulped the liquid down and felt its heat pour through her stomach. Joss she noticed was drinking whisky—neat.

'I don't want to push you out of your job, Sarah.' He squatted down beside her, so that their eyes were on a level. 'I promise you that.'

He was lying, Sarah thought dismally, but she could hardly accuse him of wanting her to leave because they had once been lovers. That would be to tread on far too uncertain ground and if she wasn't careful he would trap her into betraying the fact that she loved him.

There, she had admitted it now. . .what she had known all along, almost from the first moment he touched her. She loved Joss. . .

'Would you like me to stay here with you tonight?'

Sarah's mouth gaped open. Joss wasn't looking at her, but contemplating the contents of his glass.

'I'd sleep here on the sofa, of course,' he added tightly. 'I was only thinking you might not want to be alone.'

How right he was. . . She could have gone home to Jane and Ralph of course. . .but, of course, she recollected, they weren't back from their holidays and even if they had been home, Sarah knew she couldn't have faced their concern and anxiety right now. . .and she certainly could not face a night in her flat alone.

She closed her eyes, nodding her head weakly. 'Yes, please.'

'Right. It's four o'clock now. Why don't you go and have that bath you wanted, and I'll make us both something to eat. I promise you I'm not going to touch you, Sarah,' he added gently as he stood up. 'You have my word on that.'

She believed him. What possible desire could he have to touch her anyway? They had been lovers once; and although he had told her then that he didn't go for one-night stands, there were enough eager women in his life to ensure that he would be the last man to need to force himself on any woman. And then there was his relationship with Helene.

'Can you make it to the bathroom?'

She was sorely tempted to shake her head and give in to the pleasure of having him carry her there but instead, she struggled to sit up, sliding her feet to the floor.

She knew he was monitoring her shaky progress towards the door; she knew that if she started to fall or faint, he would catch her, and the dismal thought struck her that it was torture to be so wrapped up in his care and concern and to know that it would only be hers for tonight.

He followed her into the bedroom, stopping at the door. 'Don't lock the bathroom door, Sarah,' he told her quietly. 'The combination of the shock and that brandy. . .I'll give you half an hour, okay? If you're not out by then. . .'

Mechanically taking clean underwear from her drawer, and a casual lemon flying suit to go over it, Sarah went into her small bathroom. As she stripped off her robe, shuddering distastefully as it dropped to the floor, she reflected that it was just as well she had stayed in London at the weekend and had re-stocked her 'fridge. Joss would have no trouble finding them something to eat.

He was a complex man, she thought hazily seconds later, relaxing in the warm, scented water of her bath. As a lover, even her untutored body had recognised his skill, his enjoyment of and pleasure in her femininity. She had seen his anger. . .known that his sharp mind was working against her and even feared him because of it. . . and now she was seeing yet another side to him. . .a caring compassion which she sensed he would have extended to any woman in the same situation she had been in.

Joss was as far away from the truth as he could be if he really thought she feared he might approach her sexually, Sarah thought wryly. What really terrified her was that she might betray herself to him! And that was what had terrified her all along. She had known when she crept out of his bed that fatal morning that she was leaving more than her innocence behind her; that she had lost something to him of far more importance than mere virginity. She had loved him then. . . and that love had only gone on growing, she acknowledged. She glanced over the edge of the bath and saw her ruined bra. Revulsion shuddered through her as she felt David's greedy, hurting fingers on her breast. She picked up the soap and started lathering her skin with despairing urgency. . .trying to wash away the touch of him. There were bruise marks forming on her breast already and her flesh hurt.

'Ten minutes, Sarah. . .'

She heard Joss shout, and then the sound of her bedroom door closing behind him.

She got out of the bath, drying herself briskly, wincing as she saw the puffiness round her mouth where David had slapped her.

Her flying suit was last year's and comfortable. She was too tired to bother with fresh make-up or to do more than stroke her brush through her long hair. She looked dreadful, she thought wryly, studying her reflection momentarily in her bedroom mirror. No competition for Helene at all.

'Good timing, I was just coming to fetch you.'

Joss was standing in the doorway to the kitchen. He had discarded his jacket and his shirt was unbuttoned at the throat.

'Omelette suit you?' he asked lightly. 'It's all ready, it won't take a moment to cook.'

'Lovely.'

There was no room in Sarah's tiny flat for a dining table and she normally ate either in the kitchen or off a tray on her knees. Joss had obviously opted for the latter; she could see the trays on the kitchen counter.

'Go and sit down,' he told her gently, adding, 'how do you feel?'

'Shocked, but as though it was all somehow unreal,' she told him wryly. 'Even now I can't believe that David—'

'Stop thinking about it,' Joss ordered her. 'By the way I've taken the liberty of opening a bottle of wine.'

Wine? Sarah's nose wrinkled. She hadn't realised she had any. She drank so rarely herself and entertained in the flat so little it was something she rarely bought, and then she remembered that an author had given her half-a-dozen bottles the previous Christmas. She had pushed them to the back of one of her kitchen cupboards, and she was surprised that Joss had managed to unearth them.

'White, luckily,' he announced ten minutes later, placing a tray in front of her, a deliciously fluffy omelette heaped on to her plate.

He poured them both a glass, and then returned to the kitchen for his own tray.

'This place must seem like a mousehole to you after Houghton House,' Sarah commented wryly.

'It reminds me of my reporting days. I've lived in much worse than this, believe me. . .'

'What made you give it up, reporting I mean?'

As though he sensed her need to be distracted from her thoughts he responded to her question seriously. 'I got tired of all the travelling. I wanted more from life than to live constantly among strangers. After a while it makes you feel as though you're living in a glass bubble. . .as though you're not properly in contact with the rest of the human race.'

'So you've exchanged the glamour of being a foreign correspondent for village life. Quite a contrast.'

'Maybe. But it's what I wanted. . .I think most human beings at heart have a deep-seated need for their own place, a home base.'

'Mmm. . . You know as a teenager I always longed to live in Houghton House myself,' she admitted dreamily. 'I fell in love with the house when I was twelve, and I've remained faithful to it ever since.' She laughed as she said it, glimpsing a strange expression in his eyes.

'And are you the faithful type in everything, Sarah?' he asked her softly. 'Your heart once given, given for ever?'

She knew he was just making idle conversation, trying to help her to relax, but still she responded seriously, as though the words were compelled out of her. 'Yes. Yes. . .I am. . . The trouble is that these days most people don't want that sort of love. It's too heavy a burden' She thought fleetingly of Helene. She was divorced, like so many thousands of others.

Joss was looking at her. He was delving too deeply into her most personal thoughts, she thought in panic, learning too much about her.

'Tell me about your childhood,' she demanded. 'Where were you brought up?'

'In Lancashire,' he responded promptly. 'My father owned and ran a small printing business there. He and my mother emigrated to Australia five years ago when my sister married out there. They all live near Sydney. . .'

'You must miss them.'

She was thinking how much she had missed her own parents, how much she would miss Jane if she and her family ever moved far away. . .

'A little, but there are such things as planes and bear in mind that I'd been something of a roamer myself for several years before they left. Want another glass of wine?'

'I've already had three,' Sarah protested. In

point of fact, she was feeling pleasantly relaxed not to say slightly tipsy.

Joss glanced at his watch. 'There's a programme I'd like to see on TV in ten minutes. Would you mind?'

'No...you go ahead,' she invited him. 'What is it?'

'Oh, just a chat show, but they're interviewing an American author who I happen to know is looking for new English publishers. Henry Blake...you might have heard of him.'

Sarah had. 'Oh yes. He writes those books about the pyramids and outer space, doesn't he?'

Joss's mouth twitched slightly. 'That's one was of describing them,' he agreed gravely. 'He has a very large following...and he puts forward an extremely convincing argument.'

'Do you believe what he writes then?' Sarah challenged.

'I didn't say that.' He got up, picking up both their trays and disappearing into the kitchen, returning a few minutes later with two mugs of coffee.

'Mmm...it's lovely to be waited on like this,' Sarah told him. 'You're going to make someone a wonderful husband...' The words were out before she could stop them. It was the kind of teasing comment she might have made to any of her unmarried male friends in the same circumstances and yet for some reason the words hung uneasily on the air. For some reason? Liar, Sarah chided herself, you know damn well there's only one person you'd want to see him married to. . .

'Mmm. . .well when I get round to it I know where to come for a recommendation, don't I? Doesn't your sister spoil you when you visit her?' he added lightly, getting up again to turn on the television.

'She tries to, but it's a bit difficult for her with three children under five to look after,' Sarah told him, 'especially in view of the fact that they're triplets.'

It struck her that for a moment Joss had gone slightly paler. 'My God. . .do they run in your family?'

Sarah laughed. 'No. . . Jane had appendicitis when she was thirteen. The operation blocked her fallopian tubes. She had to have an operation and fertility drugs before she could conceive. The doctor warned her she might have twins. Three instead of two was an extra bonus. . .'

She went quiet as the programme changed, pleasurably aware of the secure bulk of Joss's body next to her own on the settee. She had kicked off her sandals and her feet were tucked up beside her. A pleasant languor filled her body. . .the wine, she thought ruefully. . . She would just close her eyes for a moment. . .

CHAPTER EIGHT

'COME on, sleepyhead, time you were in bed.'

Sarah could feel Joss's voice rumbling deep in his chest as well as hear it, but she didn't want to move from where she was. Instead, she burrowed deeper into his side, keeping her eyes closely shut.

'Sarah. Wake up. . .it's bedtime.'

Reluctantly she opened her eyes, realising that the blissful cocoon of warmth wrapped around her was Joss's arm.

She was stunned to see from the clock on the television that it was gone midnight.

'You should have woken me earlier,' she protested, muzzily. 'You must be shattered.'

'Mmm. . .I must admit the thought of sleeping on your settee isn't exactly enticing'

She couldn't see his face, and his voice was lightly amused, nothing more, but all at once Sarah was overwhelmed by a mental image of the last time the two of them had shared a bed, and suddenly she wanted that experience again more than she wanted anything else in her life; she wanted the intimacy and closeness of being held in his arms, supine and relaxed in the aftermath of love. She wanted the passionate bite of his fingers against her skin, his mouth on her body. She moaned faintly and shivered, racked by the ferocity of her need.

'Sarah, there's nothing to be frightened of now.' She felt Joss's arm tighten around her and knew that he had misunderstood the cause of her tremors.

Feeling weak and deceitful she clung to him pleading desperately, 'Joss, don't leave. . .'

'I'm not going to.' He stood up, lifting her as easily as though she were a child.

'I'll be right here outside your bedroom door. You'll be perfectly safe.'

He carried her through into her bedroom, supporting her weight while he pulled back the sheet and duvet and then placed her gently on the mattress.

'I don't want to sleep here alone. Stay with me, Joss. . .please. . .'

In the darkness his eyes gleamed like a cat's, Sarah thought absently. Every one of her senses was overpoweringly aware of him; she wanted to reach out and hold on to him. . .never let him go, but already he was disengaging himself, his expression closed and shuttered, his thoughts hidden from her.

'I can't do that, Sarah.' His voice was calm, kind almost, filling her with hurting, aching shame, as she curled away from him, turning her back on him, so that he wouldn't see the betraying shimmer of tears glittering in her eyes.

In a moment of weakness she had betrayed

herself to him, offering herself. . .and he had refused, gently, kindly. . .but it had been a rejection none the less. Pain made her whole body ache and desire for him made it burn. She had to fight not to plead with him to stay with her.

'You'll be quite safe,' he assured her, pretending not to realise that her plea had sprung from desire and not fear. 'I'll be outside. . .no one can get in.'

He was deliberately salving her pride, Sarah thought miserably, dissolving the embarrassment from the situation, but even so she was tempted to plead with him again, to beg him to stay with her, to hold her. . .

Almost as though he had read her mind he said quietly, 'I can't sleep here in this bed with you, Sarah. You must see that.'

Yes, she did see it. She saw also that whatever fleeting desire he had had for her was now gone. This was why he wanted her to leave Leichner & Holland, because he had wanted to avoid this type of situation. She wanted to cry out that she loved him, and to beg him to love her in return, but she knew that to do so would only be to embarrass him. He was not an unkind man, despite what she had thought before. He was both caring and compassionate. If he hadn't been, he would not be here with her now. . . But it wasn't his compassion she wanted, she thought fretfully, as she heard her bedroom door closing behind him, it was his love. It was the very worst kind of torment to know that he would be sleeping just the other side of that wall and that she was forbidden to be with him. She closed her eyes and let the weak tears seep beneath her lashes. It was a long time before she finally fell asleep.

'Mmm. . .well I'm glad to see you're looking very much better. I hope you feel as fit as you look. We've got a punishing schedule of work lined up for this week, including a trip to Cannes. I've got to go and see Helene about her biography. We leave tomorrow afternoon.'

Sarah was in Joss's office. Today was her first day back at work after the enforced break Joss had made her take following David's attack. She had spent the last four days with Jane and Ralph on their return from Menorca, and for once her elder sister had seemed disinclined to fuss or ask awkward questions.

Physically she felt fine, but emotionally. . . Only she knew how much she had dreaded facing Joss this morning. She had watched him with aching intensity while he was talking to her, waiting for some slight but unmistakable sign that he found her presence an embarrassing nuisance, but so far she hadn't seen one, and now he was talking about the two of them taking a business trip to Cannes.

Before she could say anything, Joss continued, 'I've had your stuff moved into the office off mine. For one thing it's larger than that cupboard you were using before and for another it's much more convenient to have my assistant within shouting distance rather than two doors away down the corridor.'

'And the women's fiction list,' Sarah asked dry-mouthed, 'Who will be looking after that?'

'You, of course,' Joss told her, frowning slightly. 'I thought I'd already made that clear, but now you will have full support from me, and I shall be the one dealing with the authors. . .'

'And my secretary?'

'Will still be your secretary,' Joss told her still frowning. 'Lindsay could hardly cope with the output from both of us. Look, Sarah,' he added coming out from behind his desk to study her, 'I thought we'd talked through this thing of yours about the transfer of responsibility being a demotion. It's no such thing. On the contrary,' he told her wryly, 'you'll find as my assistant that you gain a far wider scope of what's going on. In fact, I've got a couple of manuscripts here I'd like you to read and make notes on for me. They're novels destined for the general market if they reach publication, and I'd be very interested in a woman's view of them. Both of them are faction novels—one's written by a reporter I know very well, the other by an ex-politician.'

'What do you think of them?' Sarah asked him, picking up the manuscripts from his desk, but Joss shook his head. 'Oh no. It's your view I want. . .unbiased by whatever I might think.

'Now about this trip to Cannes,' he continued, changing the subject. 'Helene has run into problems with her biography, and she wants to talk them over with me. I was due a few days' holiday myself, and I've decided to combine the trip with a brief visit to a friend of mine who's working on a family history. He owns a small vineyard which has been passed down through the same family since the time of Napoleon, so instead of flying out to Cannes, I thought we'd drive down, and call in on him on the way. . . You don't suffer from car sickness do you?' he asked when Sarah went pale.

She shook her head, unable to explain to him that it was the thought of spending several days travelling alone with him that had driven the colour from her face. She was surprised that he was willing to endure her sole company, she thought bitterly, especially in view of her feelings for him, but then Joss was man of the world enough to know how to defuse any potentially difficult situations that might arise between them. He had proved that that night at her flat. Her face flamed suddenly as she recalled the calm way he had rejected her.

'Sarah, are you sure you're all right?' He was standing in front of her, placing cool fingers against her hot skin, making it burn even more. She jerked tensely away from him, surprised to see the way his eyes darkened and his mouth hardened.

'I'm fine,' she assured him huskily, trying to distract him by asking, 'What time did you want to leave tomorrow?'

'Well we're booked on a late evening ferry, so no later than mid-afternoon if you can make it. We won't be gone for longer than a week, I hope.' He frowned again. 'I'm extremely anxious to get this manuscript of Helene's finished. It should be quite a coup when it's published, and I'd like to see it on the shelves in time for Christmas.'

Was his anxiety solely due to getting the book finished? Sarah wondered bleakly, or was it caused by a more personal interest in the actress? Reminding herself that it was none of her business, she listened while he told her that all their travel arrangements had been made, pausing only to ask her if her passport was up to date.

For one cowardly moment she was tempted to lie and say that it wasn't, but this was now her job, she reminded herself, and she couldn't afford to lose it.

She spent the rest of the day checking through the post which had accumulated during her absence. Joss had dealt with all the urgent letters, and as she and Katy went through the rest of them Sarah grew tired of hearing her secretary sing his praises for his efficiency.

'Lucky you going to the South of France with him,' Katy commented enviously. 'I wonder if he's involved with anyone. . .'

Refusing to respond, Sarah bent her head over

the papers on her desk. She knew the answer to that all too well and was searingly jealous of the blonde-haired actress.

The first thing she did when she got back to her flat that night was ring Jane and tell her she was going to be away for a few days. Then she got out her suitcase and packed what she hoped would be enough clothes to last the duration of their travels, mainly coolly casual T-shirts, shorts and skirts, and then on an impulse she couldn't quite define she added a sheer printed silk dress that flattered her tiny waist and full breasts, telling herself even as she did so, that she was travelling with Joss on business, nothing else. . .and moreover that his head would be so full of Helene he was hardly likely to notice what she was wearing.

Her portable typewriter and a good supply of notebooks and pens were added to the small pile, her wallet checked for credit cards, even though Joss had told her he was taking care of all the financial arrangements.

Joss had told her that she needn't go in to the office in the morning, and that he would pick her up immediately after lunch, but even so Sarah deemed it wise to have an early night. She hadn't been sleeping well since David's attack, often waking during the night and then finding it hard to get back to sleep again.

Tonight was no exception and at two o'clock she lay sleepless, staring at her curtained window, longing to have Joss beside her. Like a child playing with a forbidden toy, she re-lived the night she had spent in his arms, her body tensing as it was tormented by the memory of how his touch had aroused her. It was gone four o'clock before she drifted off to sleep again, and she woke at seven feeling jaded and still tired.

Sarah spent the morning cleaning her flat. She washed and dried her hair, and on a sudden crazy impulse varnished her nails a soft pretty pink to match the cotton jeans and knit top she had elected to wear for the journey.

Unlike many redheads, she could wear pink most successfully. Catching a glimpse of herself in her mirror, suddenly aware of the way the cotton of her jeans clung to her hips and legs, and the brevity of the sleeveless boat-necked top, she was tempted to change into something more sober. Hot colour stained her skin as she visualised Joss looking at her, knowing that she had dressed in a way she hoped he would find attractive. Nonsense, she told herself curtly, she had dressed for coolness and comfort, that was all.

And yet when Joss arrived to collect her, his glance was totally impersonal. She might as well have been wearing an old sack, she realised miserably, but then what had she expected? How could she compare with a woman like Helene?

'What's this?' he asked, picking up the case with her portable typewriter. 'It weighs a ton.'

When she explained he nodded his head

approvingly. 'I meant to bring mine but the keys have been jamming and it's being repaired. Is this the lot?'

Sarah nodded her head. She had meant to offer him a cup of coffee before they set out but his manner had been so briskly distant that she had felt she ought not to. He was letting her know quite definitely that from now on they were boss and employee, she thought achingly, as she followed him out to his car. Oh, he was being pleasant enough, but there was a very obvious reserve there, a barrier that warned her that he did not wish her to trespass into more intimate territory.

Joss drove well, his large Porsche comfortable to sit in. As soon as they joined the main stream of traffic he flicked on the stereo system, the Beethoven filling the silence of the car, pleasantly soothing. . . And it served a dual purpose, Sarah thought wryly. It meant that he did not have to talk to her. It struck her that he would probably far rather not have brought her with him, and she wondered a little bitterly why he had, unless he merely wished to reinforce and underline the fact that there would be no personal involvement between them. Yes, that must be it she thought, achingly. Joss wanted to make it plain to her that what had happened between them in the past was well and truly over. Well, she would not embarrass either him or herself by throwing herself at him. . . She could take a hint as well as the next woman.

'Tired?'

They were approaching the coast and for the last few miles Sarah had been lying back in her seat with her eyes closed. This way at least she was not likely to give in to the temptation of watching Joss. He obsessed her, she admitted mentally, she could spend hours simply watching him, just absorbing the reality of him into her senses. Even with her eyes closed she was conscious of everything about him.

'Not really.' She sat up straight and forced a brief smile. 'What time do we sail?'

'Not for at least a couple of hours yet. I thought we'd stop for a meal this side of Dover—I didn't think you'd want to dine on the ferry, and once we get to the other side I want to press on as quickly as we can and I warn you, it's likely to be the early hours of the morning before we reach our destination.'

Sarah frowned, not liking the thought of Joss driving for that length of time.

'What's wrong?' he asked her.

She told him. 'Perhaps I could relieve you at the wheel for a while.'

A little to her surprise he agreed. For some reason she had half expected him to exhibit a masculine superiority towards her driving, and insist on handling the car himself.

'It's a little early to eat now,' he commented, glancing at the dashboard clock. 'Barely gone five-thirty, but if you've no objections I would prefer that we do so.'

When Sarah shook her head he continued. 'There's quite a pleasant small hotel a couple of miles down this road, where I think we'll be able to get a passable meal.'

The hotel was a couple of miles off the main road, with gardens running down to the river. It had a public bar which was already crowded when Joss escorted Sarah through it and into the small dining room which overlooked the gardens.

A little to Sarah's surprise there was no problem in serving them with a meal, although the wife of the hotel proprietor explained that because of the early hour the menu would be a little restricted. Sarah had no desire to eat a heavy meal and soon chose fresh salmon baked in herbs with an assortment of vegetables, noticing that like her Joss, too, ordered fish.

'Much lighter on the digestive system than meat,' he explained, 'and therefore, less inclined to leave one feeling lethargic.'

Both of them had opted for melon as a first course. The flesh was cool without being icy, and deliciously juicy.

The herbs in which Sarah's salmon had been baked brought out the delicate flavour of the fish. Her vegetables were crisp and tasty, and the coffee she ordered after her meal fragrant and piping hot.

Joss had cheese and biscuits, but Sarah refused anything more. They had had the dining room to themselves, although Sarah noticed that it was starting to fill up as they left.

They reached the ferry terminal just as the cars were starting to load and did not have long to wait to get on board.

The channel crossing was uneventful. Joss found them both seats in the bar, and Sarah sat back and watched the comings and goings of their fellow passengers.

Because they were not heading directly for the South of France once they had cleared Calais they had the road almost completely to themselves.

Joss pulled into the side of the road and stopped the car. 'Your turn to drive, that's if you still feel up to it?'

Sarah nodded her head, climbing out of her own seat to take the one Joss had vacated.

Ralph had taught her to drive the year she was eighteen and he had been a patient, although exacting teacher. Sarah knew that she was a competent driver, but even so she felt slightly nervous. Joss's large Porsche with its automatic transmission was not the sort of car she was used to driving, but Joss explained the mechanics of it to her patiently once he had assured himself that her seat was properly adjusted and that she could see through the rear-view mirror.

'You drive and I'll navigate,' he suggested, showing Sarah where to insert the ignition key. He shot back the cuff of the thick cotton sports shirt he was wearing to glance at his watch. 'It's just gone eight now. We'll swop over at ten, if that's all right with you?'

Although at first she was a little unsure of the unfamiliar heavy car, by the time she had travelled twenty miles in it, Sarah was beginning to relax and enjoy the feeling of power that came with the large engine. Joss was an excellent navigator, giving precise and clear instructions in plenty of time. The roads were practically deserted, and Joss was a surprisingly relaxed passenger, and unlike most of the men she knew quite content to leave her to do the driving unchecked.

At ten o'clock they stopped and swopped over. Joss drove faster than she had done, but very safely. The route they were taking was clearly marked on the map he handed to her and as he drove he explained that they were making for the Côte-d'Or wine region of France, where his friend's vineyard was.

'They produce a traditional Beaujolais— mostly *premier cru* wines although Jacques is hoping that this year's wine will be graded as *grande cru.*'

'Have you known him long?' It was ridiculous to feel this intense desire to gather up just as much information as she could to hoard like a

miser and gloat over in the empty days when Joss
himself would no longer be part of her life.

'I met him when I was working as a foreign
correspondent. Like me, he was a reporter. He had
an elder brother who had inherited the vineyard.
Renauld was killed by an Algerian bomb in Paris
eight years ago. He wasn't married, and so
Jacques inherited the vineyard and is making a
great success of it.'

'And he's still managing to find time to write
a family history as well?'

'No, it's Louise, his wife, who is really collat-
ing the information for him, although Jacques will
write the book. Château d'Anterre came to the
family as a gift from Napoleon; apparently
Jacques' ancestor was a fellow Corsican who
fought alongside Bonaparte and rose to the rank
of Marshal.'

'But for them to gain the château someone else
must have been dispossessed,' Sarah remarked.

'Yes, that's true. It's rather a romantic story
though. The tale goes that all the male members
of the family d'Anterre perished during the revol-
ution but one member of the family, a girl, was
saved and brought up in the village by her nurse.
When Jacques' ancestor came to see the château
Bonaparte had given him he saw this girl and fell
in love with her without knowing who she was.'

'Mmm. . .I suspect their marriage owed more
to French practicality than genuine romance,'
Sarah said wryly, 'but it does make a pretty story.'

She was looking at the map as she spoke and looked up, suddenly conscious of Joss's attention focused on her.

'Don't you believe in such a thing as love at first sight then, Sarah?'

Suddenly she was tongue-tied. What could she say? 'I suppose it can happen,' she admitted reluctantly at last, hoping that he wouldn't guess the reason for her burning cheeks and trembling hands.

'But you yourself have never experienced it?'

Why was he goading her like this? He must know by now how she felt about him. Luckily before she was obliged to reply they came to a crossroads where they had to turn off the autoroute they had been travelling along, and by the time she had finished giving Joss directions, he seemed to have forgotten his earlier question.

At some time or another, Sarah couldn't have said when, sleep overcame her, and it became increasingly hard to fight against the hypnotic hum of the engine and the overpowering desire to close her eyes.

She fought against doing so, but the struggle became too much for her. Her head slumped to one side and came to rest against Joss's shoulder but she was too deeply asleep to realise it.

'Wake up, sleepyhead, we're here. . .'

Sarah was having the most delicious dream. She was asleep in Joss's bed, Joss's voice a vibrant purr against her ear. She wriggled and muttered a protest, not wanting to abandon her dream.

'Sarah. . .wake up.' He was shaking her now.

Unwillingly, Sarah opened her eyes, blinking when she realised that at least some of her dream had been real. She might not be in Joss's bed, but she was curled up against his side, her head resting on his shoulder, one of his arms supporting her as his other hand gently shook her.

'You shouldn't have let me sleep for so long,' she protested. 'You must be exhausted.' She struggled to pull away from his shoulder, wondering why his mouth should tighten so ominously but before he could say anything light streamed out of the door suddenly opened in the building ahead of them. Apart from realising they were in an enclosed courtyard, Sarah could see very little of their surroundings, but the man who came out to greet them was typically French. Dark and wiry with mobile features, and dark brown eyes that caressed her with warm sensuality, he exclaimed in English:

'Joss. . .*mon ami*. . . who is this lovely lady you bring with you. . .?'

'Hands off, Jacques,' Joss drawled, getting out of the car and embracing his friend. 'Sarah is strictly out of bounds. . .'

'So.' Amusement crinkled fine lines around his eyes as Joss went to help Sarah out of the car. She felt stiff after travelling for so long and she stumbled against him, her heart pounding with fierce excitement as his fingers bit into her waist and she felt the warmth of his breath against her skin.

'Louise begs to be forgiven but she has already retired,' the host told them as he escorted them inside. 'My wife, Louise, is *enceinte*. . . how do you say. . .with child,' he explained to Sarah, 'and in these last few weeks she tires very easily.'

'What are you hoping for this time, Jacques. . . another boy?'

They were in a very traditional and enormous French kitchen of cavernous proportions, everything in it shining clean. A simple supper of bread and cheese was laid out on the well-scrubbed table, a bottle of wine opened next to it.

'*Non*. . . *non*. . . I already have two sons. . .this time I should very much wish to have a daughter. . .and Louise also, although we shall be happy with whatever *le bon dieu* sends us. But what about you, Joss?' Jacques teased his friend. 'Is it not time you were producing sons of your own? What do you say, Sarah?' Jacques asked Sarah with a liquid smile. 'Do you not think Joss would make a good papa. . .?'

Pain seized her heart in a cramping grip, unwanted images of Joss holding a child with Helene's fair hair and delicate features tormenting her mind. It astounded her that she should experience this primitive, driving need to conceive his child herself; the strength of the impulse so strong that she could actually feel the ache of loss inside her because she knew it was impossible. Why didn't Joss explain to his old friend that she was simply his assistant? It was plain to Sarah that Jacques had misread the situation and thought that there was a much more intimate relationship between them.

'I'm afraid Sarah is rather tired,' she heard Joss saying when she made no response. 'It's been a long drive.'

'But, of course. Let me show you to your room. And you, Joss. . .do you too wish to seek your bed, or will you join me in a late supper and perhaps a discussion of the kind we used to have when we were correspondents together?'

'Supper sounds a great idea,' Sarah heard Joss saying. 'I'll go out and get our bags before you show Sarah to her room.'

He was gone only briefly, returning carrying two cases, and then Sarah was following her host down what seemed like miles of passages, and then up several flights of stairs until he stopped outside a heavy wooden door.

'We have put you and Joss in the Tower suite—separate rooms I'm afraid and neither of them large enough for a double bed, but there is a connecting door either side of your shared bathroom. It was Louise's idea to put you in here. She thought you would like the view. . .'

Scarlet cheeked and embarrassed, Sarah waited for Joss to explain that they were not lovers, but to her surprise, he simply shouldered open the door and dropped her suitcase inside it, emerging again to say lightly, 'Sweet dreams, Sarah,' and then, dropping a brief kiss on the corner of her mouth, he turned to follow Jacques to another door, and having deposited his case, followed their host back downstairs.

Thoroughly bemused, Sarah wandered into her room. As Jacques had said it was only small, but completely round and she realised with a tiny thrill of delight that she was in a tower room. Another door led out of the room and she opened it to discover a bathroom on the other side, with a door in the opposite wall which she guessed must lead into Joss's room. She didn't open it, locking the door on her own side, and running a bath. She suspected that it would be quite some time before Joss came to bed, and she had no fears that he would disturb her when he did. Probably he hadn't corrected Jacques' mistaken assumption that they were lovers because he didn't want to embarrass his friend, and after all they were only staying the one day. Tomorrow evening they would be continuing their journey to Cannes, and she very much doubted that they would be given adjoining rooms in Helene's villa!

'Sarah, wake up!'

Sarah opened her eyes reluctantly, blinking in the strong morning sunlight, totally disorientated for several seconds, filled by a tidal wave of bliss as she looked up into Joss's eyes.

'Joss. . .' Her voice was sleepily sensual, her pleasure at discovering him there too intense to be concealed.

He was only wearing a towelling robe tied loosely round the waist and she longed to reach up and slide her hands into its deep vee opening and caress the tanned warmth of his skin.

'Sarah, you locked the bathroom door on my side last night and I can't get in to shower.'

Joss's curt words brought her back to reality with brutal speed. Immediately she cringed back from him, horrified by how close she had come to thoroughly embarrassing them both. Another second and she would actually have been touching him. . .caressing him. . .

'I'll go and shower now,' Joss said curtly as he stepped back from her. 'Give me fifteen minutes and then you can have the bathroom. I thought I'd better warn you that I was using it.'

No, he wouldn't want her walking in on him, Sarah thought achingly, her mind tormenting her with mental images of his naked body.

In the end she waited for half an hour before getting out of bed and opening the bathroom door.

The room was empty but the tangy fragrance of Joss's cologne clung aromatically to the air. She was assailed by such a wave of longing that she had to blink away weak tears. She didn't know which was worst, being close to him or being away from him; both, in their differing ways, were acute forms of torment.

The day passed quickly, although Sarah did not see much of Joss. He spent most of it with Jacques, discussing his book, while Louise entertained Sarah.

In her eighth month of pregnancy, she complained to Sarah that she was beginning to feel the summer heat a trial. A pretty, smiling brunette, Sarah felt an instant kinship with her and it was no hardship to spend the morning in her company.

The vineyard was very much a business concern, she explained to Sarah, adding that at this time of the year, lunch was a very scrambled casual affair, and that normally Jacques ate his outside in the vineyards with his men.

They talked about the work she had done on Jacques' book, and Sarah found herself wishing she could spend longer with her.

'Have you known Joss long?' she asked, when lunch was over.

'Only a few weeks.' It made Sarah feel guilty to know that Louise thought of them as an established couple when in fact they were no such thing.

'He's a very attractive man—I've always thought so, and not just because of his looks. It is not often one meets such a truly romantic Englishman and Joss is very romantic, I think.

That is why he has not married before now. He once told me he was waiting for a very special woman; that he wanted to fall deeply and completely in love and that nothing else would do. I'm so glad it isn't going to be Helene. He brought her here once but I didn't like her. At the time he seemed very involved with her, but obviously now—' She paused obviously not wanting to embarrass her, but Sarah was beyond that— Louise was so wrong. Joss cared nothing for her. And Helene?

Tears stung the back of Sarah's throat. Was Joss deeply and completely in love with Helene? Perhaps not in the sense that Louise meant; but he certainly desired her, which was more than he felt for her.

They left the château late in the afternoon, with Louise and Jacques both commanding them to visit them again soon.

'What did you think of them?' Joss asked Sarah as they drove away.

It struck her as an odd question for him to ask her, after all what could her opinion of his friends matter to him. Even so she replied honestly. 'I liked them both, especially Louise. . . How long will it take us to reach Cannes?' she asked him, changing the subject.

'It will be late tonight before we get there, but that shouldn't bother Helene, she's very much a night person.'

CHAPTER NINE

SARAH discovered just how true that statement was when they arrived at Helene's villa in what appeared to be the middle of a party.

The villa was several miles outside Cannes itself, set into the hillside, and would have spectacular views of the sea, Sarah suspected as she wearily allowed Joss to help her out of the car. Unlike her he seemed completely fresh and untired; as vigorously masculine as ever. A fact which Helene seemed to appreciate as she appeared in front of them, wearing a clingy silk dress that moulded the curves of her breasts and clung seductively to her long legs.

Watching her run into Joss's arms, Sarah had to turn away to hide her pain. Jealousy ripped through her with the violence of spiked talons tearing at her insides, leaving burning trails of fire.

'Joss, darling, at last. . . Mmm. . .you look divine.'

It was impossible for Sarah to drag her gaze away from the pouting red mouth caressing Joss's, even though she longed to do so.

'You must come and meet Harry—he's offering me the most marvellous part in his new film.'

'In a minute. . .' Joss disentangled himself from Helene's embrace and turned back to Sarah. 'Sarah's dead on her feet, Helene. . .if someone could show her to her room.'

For the first time Helene deigned to notice her presence, and Sarah was weakly conscious of the contrast they must present, Helene glowing vibrantly with life, her skin tanned and sleek; her make-up and hair immaculate, while in direct contrast, she looked pale and washed out, her hair lank, and her face white with tiredness. No wonder Helene was looking so triumphant, although she had scowled faintly on first seeing that Joss wasn't alone.

'Oh, yes. . .your little assistant. She's sharing a room with one of the maids. I'll get someone to take her to it. You're right, Joss,' Helene added with an acid trill of laughter. 'She looks completely washed out. . .'

Silently digesting the status to which she had been reduced, Sarah was left to her own devices, while Helene whisked Joss away.

It was almost half an hour before a young girl came up to her and touched her apologetically on the arm.

'You are the assistant of Monsieur Howard?' she asked and when Sarah nodded her head, she added, 'Please to come this way.'

The room Sarah was to share with one of the maids was barely large enough to hold the two single beds and narrow chest of drawers that were its only furniture, but Sarah was too tired to care about the paucity of her surroundings. The only bitter thought that did cross her mind as she prepared for bed was to wonder where Joss was sleeping. With Helene? Stop it, she warned herself, stop thinking like that, it's no business of yours.

The maid whose room she was sharing spoke as little English as Sarah did French, but even so Sarah found her a friendly girl. The household staff rose at six, she explained to Sarah in the morning when her alarm had woken both of them.

Wide awake once the girl had gone about her duties, Sarah went in search of the bathroom she had been shown last night. The staff's quarters were right at the top of the four-storey villa, in what must once have been attics, the bathroom antiquated but scrupulously clean.

Having showered and dressed Sarah made her way downstairs and out into the gardens of the villa, empty at this early part of the day apart from a couple of gardeners working silently on the flower beds.

As she had suspected last night, the villa commanded a breathtaking view of the Mediterranean, a panorama of wooded slopes, pastel-painted villas, and then the deep dense blue of the sea stretching out below her.

Joss had explained to her that Helene was hiring the villa for the summer, and looking at the size of it, Sarah guessed that it must be costing the actress a small fortune. The thronging crowd that had met her tired and confused gaze last night was missing this morning; a solitary male seated under one of the striped umbrella'd tables by the pool apparently engrossed in some papers he had spread out on the table in front of him.

Nevertheless he must have heard because he lifted his head and turned it in Sarah's direction, frowning slightly as he looked at her.

Sarah ventured a brief smile, and offered a tentative 'Good morning.'

'Hi, there. . .I thought I had the place to myself at this time of day. I haven't seen you around before, have I?'

'No, we only arrived last night.' Sarah introduced herself and learned that her companion's name was Harry Weinberger.

She recognised it instantly. This must be the film director Helene had mentioned to Joss the previous night.

'So what brings you here? It isn't like Helene to welcome feminine competition.' His rather full mouth twisted slightly, the cool blue eyes flickering appreciatively over Sarah's slim, jean-clad legs.

He was older than Joss. . .somewhere in his late forties, but there was an earthy attractiveness about him that Sarah suspected few women would be immune to. It wasn't so much his physical looks, she thought watching him, it was more the aura of power that clung to him, an almost

tangible awareness of himself as a man. That aura
of power would be very attractive to her sex, and
she could well understand why Helene had been
so cock-a-hoop about the role he had promised
her in his new film.

They chatted for several minutes, although
Sarah did not volunteer any information as to
what she was doing at the villa. A natural inborn
caution urged her to say nothing about Helene's
book—she had no wish to fall foul of the actress
by discussing her private affairs behind her back.

'I normally eat my breakfast round about now,'
Harry announced, glancing at his watch. 'Helene
never makes an appearance before lunchtime, and
so if you want something to eat, I suggest you
join me. Am I right in thinking you arrived with
Helene's latest male acquisition?' he questioned,
watching Sarah sharply.

Sarah turned slightly away from him so that
he wouldn't see the agony in her eyes.

'Yes. . . Joss is my boss,' she admitted colour-
lessly.

'Your boss?'

She could hear the curiosity beneath the trans-
atlantic drawl, and suspected that he was about
to question her further.

'Thanks for the offer of breakfast,' she interrupted quickly, 'but after all that driving down
here yesterday I feel like stretching my legs. If
you'll excuse me I think I'll walk down to the
village. . . It isn't very far, is it?'

'Only a couple of miles, not that there's very much down there. I'm going into Cannes later this morning. I'll give you a lift there if you like.'

'Thank you, but I'll have to check with Joss.'

It was a good excuse to escape on, although as she hurried away from the villa, Sarah wasn't really sure why she should have felt any need to escape. Harry Weinberger was an urbane, sophisticated man, and hardly one who was likely to be interested in her, but there had been a certain look in his eyes as he studied her slender figure that had set alarm bells ringing in her brain. Who knew, he might even have thought she had deliberately sought him out. As a film director he had no doubt developed a certain degree of cynicism towards her sex, Sarah reflected absently as she set off in the direction of the village.

As Harry had told her there was nothing much there, but the mouth-watering smell of freshly baked croissants filtering out from the pâtisserie proved far too tempting for her to resist, and a warm wooden bench seat beneath the plane trees in the small dusty square proved a fascinating spot to sit down and consume the croissant she had just bought, as she watched the villagers go about their daily business.

Her enjoyment of the scene in front of her was heightened by her reluctance to return to the villa, but she could not stay here for ever, she reminded herself. Sooner or later she was going to have to face up to the reality of Joss and Helene as a couple—as established lovers.

Reluctantly she got to her feet and began the long walk back to the villa.

The first person she saw as she walked down the villa's drive was Joss. He was pacing the drive frowning, the taut movements of his body indicative of a pent-up, ferocious tension. He was dressed in cream cotton jeans and a thin, short-sleeved shirt, and Sarah's heart leapt betrayingly into her throat as she simply stood and stared at him, avidly drinking in the sight of him. . .the way the heavy cotton clung to the long lines of his thighs. . .the way his hair grew thick and dark into his nape.

He turned round and saw her and his frown deepened. He didn't look like a man who had just spent the night making love she thought heart-breakingly, feeling the waves of tension beating out of him even from several yards away.

'There you are. Just where in hell have you been?' he demanded harshly, striding towards her. 'I've turned this damned place upside down looking for you.'

'I walked down to the village.' To her consternation Sarah found that she was flushing, guiltily conscious of the fact that she was here ostensibly to work, and that she was not a free agent. As a palliative she offered without thinking, 'I wouldn't have gone out, but Harry Weinberger told me Helene never gets up before lunchtime.'

Instantly, she was aware of her mistake.

'So?' Joss demanded icily.

What could she say? Luckily Joss seemed disinclined to press for her response, instead hurrying her towards the villa. 'I'm seeing Helene at twelve to talk to her about her book. I want you in on the meeting to take notes.' He frowned and came to an abrupt halt. 'And just how did you get so pally with Weinberger?'

'He was out by the pool this morning when I walked past. We got talking.'

'Did you now? Well you'd better not let Helene catch you just talking to him. She considers Harry to be very much her own private property.'

Joss was still frowning, and Sarah felt a wave of sympathy for him wash over her. Could he be jealous of the film director? If so, she knew exactly how he must be feeling. She wanted to reach out and touch him. . .to offer him some sort of comfort, but she knew she daren't let herself come into physical contact with him. It might prove too much for her shaky self-control.

In the event it was half-past-twelve before Helene deigned to see them. She received them—and that was the only word Sarah could use to adequately describe the languorous manner in which she lay on a silk-covered chaise-longue—in the pretty sitting room off her bedroom, her voluptuous body sheathed in pure silk satin lounging pyjamas, her hair and make-up immaculate, but her expression petulant and bored, anger sparkling in her eyes the moment she saw Sarah.

'Joss, darling, surely we don't need your little assistant here. . .I was looking forward to having you to myself,' she pouted.

Sarah couldn't look at Joss. Instead she started to move back to the door, but he stopped her, fastening hard fingers round her wrist. 'Sarah stays, Helene,' he said coolly. 'I need her to make notes. Now. . .what was the problem you needed to discuss so urgently?'

Helene pouted, but after another acid look at Sarah she started explaining. 'I wanted to do a chapter about my relationship with John Vincent—he directed me in my first film, and everyone said that he exploited me, paying me a flat fee instead of offering me a percentage. . . Of course the whole world knows that he's gay and that he dislikes attractive women. He was madly jealous of me at the time because Gray was so attracted to me, and he wanted Gray himself. . .I want to put all this in the book, Joss, but Richard doesn't agree.'

'He's quite right,' Joss told her after a few moments' silence. 'You don't want to be landed with a libel or slander suit, Helene. . .'

The actress's eyes flashed, her mouth hardening with temper. 'It's my book, Joss,' she said angrily, 'and I'll put in it what I damn well want to. . . . If you don't publish it, someone else will. In fact—'

'Stop threatening me, Helene.' Sarah marvelled that Joss could keep so calm. 'You asked me for my advice and I'm giving it to you.'

'But can't you see? It would serve John right if I exposed him. . .made him look the pathetic little creep that he is.' Ugly patches of colour darkened Helene's skin, suddenly making her look all of her thirty-odd years. 'He kept me out of the latest Harding film you know. . .and everyone knows that it's bound to get an Emmy. That part was made for me, but he gave it. . .I'm going to put that chapter in my book, Joss. . .and you're not going to stop me. Oh, Joss, I thought you'd be on my side,' she cried, suddenly abandoning her anger and getting off the chaise-longue, to cling to Joss's side, curling her nails into his skin.

Sarah wanted to look away but she could not. The sight of the actress clinging to Joss exercised a horrible sort of fascination over her, compelling her to watch, no matter how much the sight tormented her.

'I am, but you can't seem to see it.' Unbelievably Joss was now smiling rather wryly. 'I do understand your desire for revenge, Helene.' Was that really a certain cynical dryness she heard in his voice, or was she imagining things, Sarah wondered? 'But you haven't thought of the high price you might have to pay. Vincent will most definitely sue if anyone publishes what you want to write.'

'I don't believe I'm hearing this, Joss.' Helene released him and started pacing the floor. 'In fact, I'm going to pretend I haven't heard it. I suggest that you take yourself and your little assistant off and have a very good think about what you've just said. . . When you've done that, I'm sure you'll see that I'm right, darling. . .'

'And if I don't. . .?'

Joss's voice was totally devoid of all expression.

'Well then, darling,' Helene told him malevolently. 'I'll just have to find another publisher, won't I?'

The rest of the day was a nightmare. Joss disappeared after their interview with Helene reappearing only after the *al fresco* lunch which was served on the patio. As on the previous evening the pool and garden area were crowded with people, all of whom seemed to greet one another as 'darling', most of them men Sarah noticed, and all of whom seemed to form an adoring court around Helene. Watching her fondle the sun-bronzed back of one young boy who, despite his arresting physical appearance, could not have been a day over twenty years old, Sarah thought it was just as well that Joss wasn't there to witness what was going on.

He reappeared during the afternoon, dressed in swimming shorts, and looking rather grim. Watching the fast, demanding crawl with which he traversed up and down the pool for a dozen or so lengths, Sarah felt her heart ache with sympathy for him. He was not a man who would find it easy to stand on one side while his lover openly demonstrated her interest in other men. Harry Weinberger was sitting with Helene now, Sarah noted, absently admiring the skill with which the older man detached the young Adonis from Helene's side, and then captured her attention for himself.

'Envying her?' She hadn't seen Joss get out of the pool, and he showered small droplets of warm water on her skin as he came to sit down beside her.

'No,' Sarah told him, with clear-eyed honesty, wondering why on earth he should think she was the slightest bit attracted to the film director, 'just admiring his technique.'

'Well, he's certainly had plenty of practice. He's just got rid of his fourth wife. . .'

'Do you think Helene will back down over the book?' Sarah asked him, wanting to distract his attention from the other couple, knowing what he must be feeling at the sight of them together.

'I doubt it. She can be very stubborn when she wants to be.'

'So what will you do?'

'I've told Helene my stance on the subject,' Joss said coolly, 'and I'm not going to change my mind—not through bloody-mindedness but because I know I'm right. If we went ahead and published the book as Helene wants to write it, John Vincent would sue us straight away, and I can't say I would blame him. Helene's letting her desire to pay him out blind her to reality, I'm afraid. . .'

'And if we lose the book and she takes it to another publisher. . .' She held her breath, knowing how much he had been depending on having the book in the shops for Christmas.

'Better to lose the book than face a law suit,' he said, shrugging easily. 'It isn't the end of the world. To be honest, now that I've read what she's done so far, I'm not very impressed. Richard, her agent, has done most of the work for her, but in reality it's nothing more than a lot of badly cobbled together gossip. Even so it would have sold after some work by a good ghost writer. However, we can't win 'em all. Still I suppose I'd better go and see if I can talk some sense into her.' He got up, his body sleek and supple, already a warm brown. She longed to reach out and touch him; to run her hands up over the silken planes of his skin, to. . . Gulping painfully, she closed her eyes and settled back in her lounger, mentally comparing her own very respectable chain-store bikini to the far more daring garments the other women were wearing. Most of them were bare-breasted, with bodies that spoke of endless hours in gyms and working out.

Against her will, she glanced across to where Joss was sitting with Helene and Harry Weinberger. Helene was stroking the director's bare forearm, leaning into his body, laughing up at him, her every movement calculated to make

Joss jealous, Sarah recognised, knowing that this was the actress's way of punishing him for defying her. She didn't know how Joss could stand it, and she marvelled at and admired his self-control.

A lesser man would have given in. . .but Joss wouldn't, she reflected. Nothing would deflect him from his decision, and she suspected that Helene would not be pleased about that. She was a woman who was used to commanding the adoration and obedience of her men, but Joss was not cast in that mould.

Her long fingers curled round Harry Weinberger's thigh, her eyes narrowing in sexual pleasure as she stroked the firm flesh. See, she seemed to be saying to Joss. . .see what you are missing, what pleasure I could give you. . .but Joss seemed to be oblivious to her manoeuvres, Sarah thought mechanically, knowing exactly how she would feel if she was there in his place, watching him openly and very sensually caressing someone else while she was at his side.

Unable to bear any more Sarah got up and went inside. Her small room at the top of the house was hot and stuffy, but at least up there she didn't have to endure the sight of Helene tormenting Joss—and enjoying every minute of it.

The stuffiness in her room made her head ache, but Sarah was reluctant to go back outside. She found some magazines that belonged to the maid and flicked idly through them, wishing with all her heart that Joss had left her behind.

The sound of footsteps in the corridor outside made her frown and put the magazine down, her frown changing to surprise as Joss thrust open the door and walked in.

'Good God,' he exclaimed looking round the tiny room. 'It's like an oven in here. Can't you open the window?'

Sarah shook her head. 'No, they're all screwed down. Perhaps these rooms were once nurseries. Did you want me for something?'

'Yes—we're leaving—just as soon as you're ready,' he told her tersely.

'Leaving!' Sarah stared at him. 'Have you. . .? Has Helene. . .?'

'The answer to both those questions is "no",' he told her with dry irony. 'Helene it seems is more interested in securing a part in Weinberger's new film than discussing her book, so we might as well leave.'

Poor Joss. Sarah could imagine how he must be suffering, forced to watch Helene flirting with Harry Weinberger. No wonder he wanted to leave.

'It won't take me long to pack,' she assured him quickly. 'I'll meet you downstairs, in say. . . half an hour.'

'Fine. I'll go and give our hostess the good news. I'm quite sure our presence won't be missed.'

He was hiding his bitterness well, even managing to sound faintly derisive, but Sarah wasn't deceived.

Helene didn't even bother to see them off, and Sarah felt she could well understand the reason for the tension hardening the bones of Joss's face as they drove away.

It wasn't until they were clear of Cannes that he spoke to her, and then only to say briefly, 'I hope to God we can find somewhere to stay tonight. It's not going to be easy, right in the height of the season.'

His prediction proved all too accurate and it was well after ten o'clock when they eventually found rooms in a small family run *auberge* a few miles off the main tourist route, in a small village.

They would have to share a bathroom, Joss told Sarah briefly as he signed the register, but Sarah was beyond caring. They seemed to have been travelling for ever, and the long journey down to Cannes, and the tension of their stay at the villa, were now catching up on her.

'I've organised a meal for us,' Joss told her, 'but first I need a shower.' He grimaced, running his hand through his hair. 'God, I'm tired. . .'

He looked it, too. 'You use the bathroom first then,' she offered. 'I'm not too bad,' she fibbed, 'after all you're the one who's been doing all the driving.'

She gave him half an hour before going upstairs herself. The door to the bathroom they were to share was open. Joss had obviously vacated it. She was too tired herself to bother about finding anything special to wear. What did it matter anyway? Joss wouldn't notice. His mind would be on Helene.

A soft cotton dress lay at the top of her suitcase and grabbing it and clean underwear she made for the bathroom.

Her shower revived her a little, and feeling at least clean and fresh she went downstairs in search of Joss and her meal.

The small dining room was empty. Frowning slightly she went outside thinking he might be in the garden, but it, too, was deserted. On her way back into the foyer, she bumped into the proprietress, who shrugged her shoulders and looked blank when Sarah asked her in her schoolgirl French if she had seen Joss.

He must still be in his room. . .perhaps waiting for her, she realised, going back upstairs slowly.

His bedroom was opposite hers, the door slightly open. Sarah tapped on it and walked in, coming to an abrupt halt, his name dying on her lips as she saw Joss sprawled out across the bed on his stomach, the brief towel wrapped round his hips his only covering.

Her entrance had obviously woken him, and he turned his head, staring groggily up at her. Something in the way she was watching him must have betrayed her because almost instantly the grogginess disappeared from his eyes to be replaced by a glittering febrile intensity.

His glance swept her from head to toe, leaving her skin burning. He got up off the bed, the same, but suddenly different, dangerous in a predatory unleashed way that trailed flutters of alarm down her spine. This was not the Joss whose control she had envied and admired as he sat watching Helene flirt with Harry Weinberger. This was a man whose emotions were most definitely not under any sort of control at all she recognised numbly as he came towards her.

'What is it, Sarah?'

How silky and soft his voice was, but danger-ous, too, setting her pulses thudding in primitive warning.

'I came. . .to tell you that our meal was ready.'

'Did you. . .but it wasn't food you were think-ing about just now was it, Sarah?' He had drawn level with her now and she could smell the musky male scent of his skin. She wanted to turn and leave the room. . .to escape from the danger she could feel closing in around her, but she simply could not move.

'You were looking at me as though you couldn't wait to feel my skin against your own. . . as though you couldn't wait to touch me.' His voice was low and faintly rasping now, making her shiver in tense reaction. She wanted to deny what he was saying. . .to escape from the humili-ation he was forcing on her, but she couldn't. She was like a helpless rabbit mesmerised by a hawk.

'Do you want to touch me, Sarah? Do you want to feel my flesh against your own? Were you remembering what it was like between us?' He laughed suddenly, a harshly bitter sound.

'Joss...please, I know why you're doing this...' Her throat hurt as she forced the words out. 'I know how you feel about Helene.' She risked a brief look at him and found that he had gone tensely still, his eyes narrowing on hers. 'I know you...'

'What is it you're trying to tell me, Sarah?' he demanded softly. 'That you're *jealous* of Helene? *Were* you jealous of her, Sarah?' he probed, closing the distance between them. 'Of this. Were you jealous of this...?'

His mouth was on her own, taking it without finesse or delicacy, his arms locking round her like bands of iron as his self-control was blasted away completely and he gave in to the tightly reined emotions she had sensed churning within him all day.

She knew she ought to resist...that it was not *her* he wanted, but the sheer sensuality of his kiss exercised its own dark power. Against her will she responded to it, her lips parting to the thrusting demand of his tongue.

His body burned against her own, his hands urgent and ungentle as he caressed her. She tried to break free of him, appalled by the sudden pressure his arms exerted on her body as he restrained her.

'Don't fight me tonight, Sarah,' he muttered against her throat. 'I need this too much to stop now. You shouldn't have come in here. . .but now that you have. . .'

His heartbeat thudded crazily into her chest, all sense and reason suspended as she found herself responding instinctively to the male lure of him. This was the man she loved. . .wanting her. . . needing her.

'Stay with me tonight, Sarah.' His mouth touched hers, lightly, less lightly, and then very fiercely as he reinforced his need. She could feel it in his body; in the hard urgency of his muscles, and in the tormenting throb of his arousal.

It was easy now to forget how he had rejected her. . .that he didn't love her, when she stood within the circle of his arms, and his mouth was slowly caressing the tender arch of her throat. Without realising she had moved she felt the smooth skin of his back beneath her palms, a long shudder of pleasure rippling through his body as she slowly caressed the supple flesh. His teeth bit gently into the vulnerable juncture of her throat and shoulder, and then again less gently, so that it was her turn to shudder and cling help-lessly to him as he eased down the zip of her dress.

She was almost feverish with the need to be rid of her clothes. She wanted to feel the satin glide of his body against her own. She wanted to touch him, to taste him. Blindly she placed her lips against the hollow of his throat, amazed and thrilled by the explosive sounds of pleasure he made beneath her tentative caress, his fingers against the vertebrae of her spine, pressing her into his body so that her breasts were flattened against his chest.

'Why the hell do you have to wear so many clothes?' He muttered the protest against her ear as he unfastened and removed her bra, holding her slightly away from him as he cupped and studied the aroused fullness of her breasts.

'I can't believe you're real.' He said it slowly, like someone caught up in a dream, his eyes dark and veiled, almost unfocused.

'Come to bed with me now, Sarah,' he muttered against her mouth, slowly drawing her towards the bed.

Sarah went unresistingly with him, letting him pull her down beside him on the bed, watching almost dreamily as he threw off his towel and removed her briefs. Her body knew his now... knew it and reacted immediately to the proximity of it, her senses already savouring the pleasures she knew were to come.

'Sarah.' Joss whispered her name against her mouth, kissing her slowly, his hand cupping her jaw, holding her beneath his mouth as it ravaged hers with increasingly urgent kisses. His heart was thudding at twice its normal rate, the heat coming off his skin burning her own. Beneath his breath he was muttering words she couldn't decipher; his hand leaving her face to travel along her throat and down to her breast, his fingertips lightly grazing her already erect nipples.

'Joss. . .' Sarah was barely aware of moaning his name as she arched eagerly beneath his hands, but she heard the hoarse note of desire in his voice as he demanded rawly, 'What is it you want, Sarah? Is it this?' His mouth touched her throat, caressing it moistly. 'This. . .?' His head dipped further, his tongue tracing slow circles against the aureole of her breasts. She was dissolving in pleasure, Sarah thought hazily, melting in those circles of fire Joss was painting on her body. She reached up towards him, dragging her nails protestingly along his shoulder, unable to endure the sensual torment of his warm mouth against her skin. Her teeth found his shoulder and bit protestingly, her body shuddering in heated delight as Joss's teeth caught against her nipple as he dragged in a deep breath.

'Do that to me again and I won't be responsible for how I react,' he muttered thickly. 'I want to feel your mouth against my skin, Sarah,' he told her huskily, 'it does things to me that I can't begin to describe. . .'

Listening to him was doing things to her that she couldn't begin to describe, Sarah acknowledged hazily. The erotic mental images he was drawing for her, were turning her blood to fire, drugging her senses. . .making her shudder in delicate response to what he was saying.

'Make love to me, Sarah.' He murmured the command with aching urgency, drawing her down against his body.

Her fingers clutched at his shoulder and then relaxed, tracing the hard muscles beneath his skin, her lips instinctively feathering light kisses along the same path. Hesitant at first, Sarah felt her confidence grow as Joss responded openly to her caresses, inviting them to become more intimate.

Her fingers touched the hard flatness of his belly and he shuddered convulsively, muttering her name, but when she drew away his hand covered hers, holding it against his body, moving it to where he throbbed demandingly.

The maleness of him beneath her hand was distinctly arousing, her stomach muscles tightening, desire flooding through her, weakening her so that she wasn't sure which of them it was who shivered.

Her need to feel the life force of him pulsing deep within her was overwhelming.

'Sarah.' Feverishly Joss caressed her body, drawing her up against him, moving against her in urgent demand. She wanted him so much. The intensity of it coiled achingly within her, exploding into liquid heat when his fingers touched the velvet moistness from which the heat radiated.

'You want me.' His voice was thick and drugged with passion, slurred faintly with an edge of masculine triumph. Beneath the open sexual desire glittering in his eyes Sarah could sense a more primitive male delight in his ability to arouse her, to reduce her to this melting, writhing mass of nerve endings that craved only one release.

And then suddenly she was sick with self-disgust. What was she doing—allowing Joss to use her as a means of relieving his frustration? He didn't want *her*. . . not in the way that she wanted him, above and beyond all other human beings. She was simply a body in his bed, a woman who he could use to forget Helene for a few brief hours.

He sensed her withdrawal immediately, his body tensing, the glitter of sexual hunger in his eyes replaced by a mingling of anger and. . .and what? she asked herself achingly. Pain? Hardly.

'What's wrong. . .?' He wasn't touching her at all now, and in fact had moved completely away from her. Treacherously her body missed the heat and pressure of his. She shivered, suddenly cold, coming down too quickly from the high plateau to which he had taken her.

'I think I'd better leave, Joss.' She made to get out of his bed, but to her surprise he reached out and stopped her. 'For God's sake, Sarah. . .' The words were strained and hoarse. She could sense him fighting for self-control and reminded herself that he had every reason to feel rage against her. She should never have allowed their lovemaking to get so far.

'Look. . .we have to talk.' He sounded surprisingly gentle, but very, very tired, as though emotionally he was drained dry. 'I promise you I won't touch you again.'

She couldn't hide her expression from him; the bleak misery that filled every part of her mind and body as she acknowledged what he was saying. Of course he wouldn't touch her again. . .he wouldn't have touched her at all if it hadn't been for Helene. Suddenly she was too miserable and exhausted to conceal the truth from him any longer. She could not go on working for him feeling the way she did about him. . .at this moment in time she simply didn't have the energy or the willpower to fabricate a suitable lie. Perhaps after all it was better to tell him the truth. After all he had never deliberately set out to hurt her. It was hardly his fault that he didn't want her love. How much easier everything would have been if there had simply been that one night between them. If they had never met again. But that wouldn't have stopped you loving him, an inner voice told her.

'Sarah, what is it?'

Wearily she told him. 'It isn't the fact that you touched me, Joss.' She shut her eyes as her throat closed on a tight ball of pain, and admitted huskily, 'Far from it. It's the fact that you were using me as a substitute for Helene. . .'

There was no mistaking the quality of the stunned silence that followed her announcement. Joss sat up and grasped her arms, pulling her half upright and snapping on the bedside lamp so that he could see her properly.

'Say that again?' he commanded thickly.

Hesitantly Sarah did so, fascinated by the way his fingers tensed into her skin, his eyes closing as he tipped his head back and swallowed deeply.

When he spoke his voice was unfamiliar, thick and clogged with a rawness that made her own pain intensify.

'Like hell! For God's sake, Sarah! I was making love to you quite simply because not to do, was driving me completely out of my mind. . . *You* are driving me out of my mind,' he underlined, shaking her and then before she could stop him dragging her into his arms, his mouth blindly searching for and finding her own.

He was kissing her. . .touching her like a man starved of any physical contact over a period of months rather than minutes, his mouth moving on hers with an absorbed intense hunger.

'I love you, Sarah. . . Surely you realise that?'

She felt the movement of his lips against her own, heard the words but could not take them in.

'Say something, dammit.' He was shaking her again, or was it he who was shaking, his face drawn and strained, his eyes almost black, burning in a face suddenly gaunt with need.

'But how can you?' She was whispering the question, reaching out to touch his face with her fingers, registering the convulsive hunger with which he pressed them to his mouth, feeling the rapid thud of his heart beneath the palm she had placed against his body to support herself.

'But how can you love me? You never. . .I thought you wanted to get rid of me. . .that I would read more than you intended into what had happened between us. . .and then there was Helene.'

'A smoke screen who I used to stop myself from frightening you off. . .and I admit, who I also used to try and make you feel jealous. Helene has never meant anything to me, Sarah. She's shallow and vain. . .the sort of woman who's more of a turn off than a turn on.'

'But that night at my flat when you stayed with me. . .when I wanted you.'

She saw the look of pain cross his face. 'Did you think I had rejected you?' He shook his head. 'You were so vulnerable that night, Sarah. . .too vulnerable. I daren't risk taking what you were offering me in case you regretted it in the morning. Suddenly, tonight I was tired of playing games, Sarah, of holding off in case I frightened you away. Whether you're ready to hear this or not, it's too late. . .I love you, Sarah. . .I fell in love with you the moment I saw you at the ball. I couldn't believe what was happening to me. . . how I felt about you—but you seemed to feel it, too. . .' He shook his head like a man coming out of a dream and Sarah felt her heart contract with love and joy.

'I told myself it was all too good to be true,

that I was going headlong into danger, but my heart wouldn't listen,' he told her wryly. 'You've no idea what it did to me when I woke up and found you gone.' His fingers traced the shape of her mouth. 'I wanted to put you through hell for that. . .for the agony you caused me.'

'But you didn't try to find me.'

He didn't deny it. 'No. . . I'd already taken too much of an emotional beating to risk any more pain. You see, Sarah, when you came to me. . . gave yourself to me the way you did I thought it was because you shared my feelings. . .I thought that when we made love we had established a rapport, a relationship, that went far beyond the merely physical. For the first time in my life I was experiencing the reality of love. . .when I woke up and found you gone I knew that reality had only been an illusion. Your very absence proclaimed more loudly than any amount of words, that you did not share my feelings. . .that what for me had been a unique experience I wanted to treasure for the rest of my life, was for you something you wanted to put behind you and hide from.'

'I had no idea you felt like that. . .I thought I was just. . .just a one-night stand.'

He grimaced faintly. 'Thanks very much. Didn't I tell you at the time that I didn't go in for them? You hurt me, Sarah, and badly. . .I was only just beginning to come to terms with what happened when I walked into Leichner & Holland and discovered—'

'Me sitting there. . .'

'Mmm. . .and obviously as embarrassed and resentful as hell to discover I was going to be a permanent feature of your working life. I almost wanted to kill you when you told me why you'd made love with me', he admitted rawly, pain reflecting in his eyes for a moment as he stared down at her.

'I was twisting the truth for self-defence,' Sarah admitted. 'Oh, Jane and I had talked about me protecting myself from David by taking a lover, but I would never have done it.' She smiled mischievously up at him. 'I saw you before the ball you know. . .I was shopping in town with Jane.'

'And?'

'And quite unconsciously I wondered what you would be like as a lover. . .I told myself it was because of what Jane and I had been discussing, but it was more than that. . . It was you, Joss,' she admitted huskily, 'although I wasn't ready to admit with my mind then what my heart was telling me. It sounds so ridiculous, falling in love with a stranger.'

'Ridiculous. . .and at times excruciatingly painful,' Joss agreed wryly, 'but nevertheless a reality.'

'Yes. That's why I ran away. . .why I left that morning. I woke up and looked at you and suddenly I was scared. I knew what we'd had wasn't enough. . .but how could I believe you would feel about me as I did about you? For all I knew you might just have wanted a light-hearted affair, and I knew I couldn't have endured that. . .it seemed safer simply to run.'

'But now I've caught you.'

'Yes.' Her voice was a breathless tremor.

'And since you're my captive, you're mine to do with as I please. . .'

'Yes.'

'To obey my every command.'

He was kissing her now, teasing, light kisses that made her forget everything but the need to cling to him and mutely demand more. . . much more.

He stopped kissing her and lifted his head to study her for a moment.

'Sarah, are you sure triplets don't run in your family?' he demanded thickly.

She laughed. . .'Quite sure.'

'Mmm. . .good.' He was kissing her again and this time it was her turn to withdraw.

'But twins do,' she teased him.

'And in mine. Nice. . .two little girls just like you. I think I'd like that.'

'Or two little boys just like you.' She said it dreamily, her body instantly responding to the touch of his hands against it, the look in his eyes turning her bones fluid.

'Is that what you want?' He whispered the question against her mouth.

'Yes, please.'

Instantly his expression changed, triumph gleaming in his eyes as he announced vigorously, 'Good. Then you'll have to marry me first. . .I'm a very conservative type you know. No wedding, no twins. . .'

'Is that right? She laughed at his expression and then said soberly, 'Joss, are you sure I'm what you want?'

'More sure than I've been of anything else in my life. I knew it the first time I saw you.'

Sarah digested his words in silence, the sincerity and depth of them driving out the last vestiges of her doubts.

Smiling at him she reached up to embrace him, loving the shudder that racked through his body when hers moved against it.

'Joss, I love you so much. . .'

'Thank God for that.'

His prosaic reception of her declaration was slightly dampening. 'I thought I was never going to hear you say it,' he told her huskily, correctly reading her expression. 'In so many words that is. . .' he teased. 'Your body has already, in the most satisfactory way possible.' He laughed as she made to hit him with a small fist, kissing her until she ceased to struggle, until there ceased to be anything other than the taste and feel of him, and then drawing her down beside him he added softly, 'But I wanted more than the response of your body, Sarah. I wanted your heart as well, your commitment. . .your love. . .'

'All that and in return all I get is a vague promise of twins. . .' She pretended to be horrified.

'That,' Joss agreed dulcetly, 'and, of course, this. . .'

Her body melted against him, her lips parting for his kiss, everything else forgotten as Joss showed her the depth and intensity of his love.

HARLEQUIN  PRESENTS®

HARLEQUIN PRESENTS
men you won't be able to resist
falling in love with...

HARLEQUIN PRESENTS
women who have feelings
just like your own...

HARLEQUIN PRESENTS
powerful passion in
exotic international settings...

HARLEQUIN PRESENTS
intense, dramatic stories that will keep you
turning to the very last page...

HARLEQUIN PRESENTS
The world's bestselling romance series!

LOOK FOR OUR FOUR FABULOUS MEN!

Each month some of today's bestselling authors bring
four new fabulous men to Harlequin American Romance.
Whether they're rebel ranchers, millionaire power brokers
or sexy single dads, they're all gallant princes—and
they're all ready to sweep you into lighthearted fantasies
and contemporary fairy tales where anything is possible
and where all your dreams come true!

You don't even have to make a wish…
Harlequin American Romance will grant your every desire!

Look for Harlequin American Romance
wherever Harlequin books are sold!

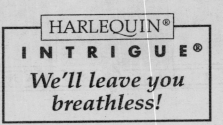

HARLEQUIN SUPERROMANCE®

...there's more to the story!

Superromance. A *big* satisfying read about unforget-
table characters. Each month we offer
four very different stories that range from family
drama to adventure and mystery, from highly emotional stories to romantic comedies—and
much more! Stories about people you'll
believe in and care about. Stories too
compelling to put down....

Our authors are among today's *best* romance writers. You'll find familiar names and
talented newcomers. Many of them are
award winners—and you'll see why!

If you want the biggest and best
in romance fiction, you'll get it
from Superromance!

Available wherever Harlequin books are sold.

Harlequin® Historical

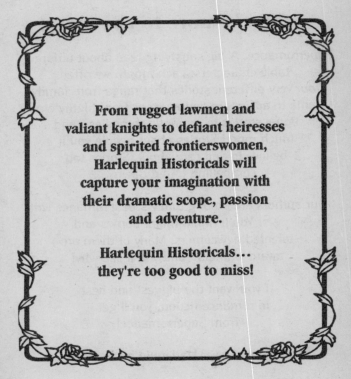

From rugged lawmen and valiant knights to defiant heiresses and spirited frontierswomen, Harlequin Historicals will capture your imagination with their dramatic scope, passion and adventure.

Harlequin Historicals... they're too good to miss!